Filtiarn

MIRANDA STORK

<u>Filtiarn</u>

Miranda Stork

ISBN-13: 978-1-909816-71-8

Moon Rose
Publishing

CHAPTER ONE

"I have to get Jenny back. I won't leave her."

The group followed Taraghlan's hurried movements as he sprinted in the direction of the castle, settling down onto the grass with uneasy expressions. Conner eased himself down to Erin on the bumpy hillside, giving a grunt as he leaned back against a tree. His joints popped in protest, a reminder of the long journey he had been on before they attempted their escape — which had been thankfully easier than expected.

Erin stared off into the distance towards Athol Castle, with a dreamy look in her eyes, lost in her thoughts. The breeze blew gently at her long strands of chestnut hair, and her hand came up to instinctively tuck them behind her ears again. Conner gave her a gentle nudge, rubbing his face against her shoulder. "What's wrong?" he asked softly, sending her a lopsided smile.

Erin shrugged, heaving a weighted sigh. "It shouldn't have ended this way. I can't believe what has happened. The war, humanity in tatters and pockets of resistance. Is it worth it? Even if we do manage to overturn everything, it will never be the same. The world will never forget. We may have to stay in hiding forever."

Lifting his head from her shoulder, Conner gave a firm nod, tensing his jaw. "I think it will make a difference," he replied. "Even if we do go into hiding, it doesn't matter. I'll have you." He turned to give her a wink, breathing in her soft scent. "It will make a difference." His eyes cooled to their usual amber as he looked out over the hill, scanning the distant horizon as though keeping wary of lycanthropes charging back up at them.

Erin raised her eyebrows before casting her sky-blue eyes to the ground, hooking her hands around her knees. "How?"

Clearing his throat, Conner closed his eyes for a moment, as though relishing the moment of being outside in the cool evening air. The breeze carried the fragrance of nearby flowers with it, and the trees filtered the sinking sun into dabbled golden spots, the atmosphere feeling more like a summer's eve with friends than the aftermath of a battle. "Try looking at it this way. Imagine you have a beautiful mirror, and it gets smashed into pieces. If you try to glue the pieces back to their frame, no matter how well you do it, it will never look the same—it will never be a mirror again. But you can glue the pieces into something else—say a mosaic—and create something new and beautiful from the pieces, even though it isn't exactly the same."

Erin grinned for the first time since she had left the castle, lighting her face and easing some of the worry and doubt that creased in her brow. *He's right. We can't recreate what was before, but it's not as though this hasn't happened before in history—it just hasn't happened on such...on such a grand scale. We can repair it though, and make something new and better. A phoenix rising from the ashes. I hope it's that easy. But of course it won't be.* The thought stayed in her mind as she glanced across to the castle again, its domineering grey stone lit gently by the pale evening sun. A bird called out somewhere off in the distance, its wavering cry carrying through the still air, a sweet, desperate cry to the others it no longer heard. "I agree—in theory. But I don't think it is as simple as that this time—it isn't a mirror we've broken, it's all of mankind. It's going to take more than a new frame and a bit of superglue."

Conner shook his head again, smiling knowingly. "If there is one thing I have learned about mankind, and seen over the years, it's this—humanity will always bounce back. More than any other creature—including werewolves—they have always returned stronger through adversity." Then he sighed, and his expression turned sad. "However, I fear that there are still those who might try and aim for that. I'm regretting a decision I made back at the Black Tower."

Erin's heart stilled at his words, and she folded her arms over her chest, the warm breeze turning cooler at his words. Scanning his face for clues, she jerked her head in response. "Who do you mean? What decision?"

"My mother. When I met her back at the Black Tower, she helped me remove the curse she put upon us, so in return I let her keep her life. I'm wondering now if it was such a good idea."

Demitri and Matthew both glanced up at his words from across the clearing, gazing at one another before Matthew ventured, "May I ask why?"

Giving a snort, Conner snapped his liquid amber eyes open and grinned wryly at his friend. "Why did I let her live, or why am I worried? I guess it's the same answer, either way. When she took the curse off, she did it so...readily. Why go through all the centuries of hatred just to remove it so easily? I was suspicious when she did it, but I was too worried about Erin. Perhaps some small part of me thought she would take my gesture as a sign of good faith, and disappear. But I don't know now." He let his hand fall to the grass by his side, running his fingers through it and slicing a nail through the stalks, letting the fresh smell burst into the air. "Now I wonder if she did it because she was planning something worse." A daisy head was popped off as he ended his words on a rough grunt.

Getting to her feet, Erin ran a hand through her long hair, twisting it back into a ponytail as she pursed her lips tightly. "I wouldn't trust her. But it's not your fault, I wouldn't ask you to kill your own mother." Her eyes narrowed, and she turned a burning glare to the others. "I might though. I've remembered a few things since waking up. It's...weird. It's like I've been leading a double life, but I'm getting memories of both, slowly." She chuckled, striding across the glade and fixing her gaze on the castle below. "I remember being an Alpha. It's coming back, in bits and pieces." Her frame stilled, and she curled her hands tightly, mind racing as flickering images whizzed through at breakneck speed. It was as though a dam had burst since she had the enchantment removed, and anything she had ever done in her two-thousand-plus years was sinking into her soul again, jigsaw pieces finally falling into place. Her voice cold and hard, she rasped, "I remember your mother, Conner. I remember how broken she was when Filtiarn left. But I also remember how she screamed blue murder at me, swore she would make me pay. I remember how she took control of the pack when I wasn't there. She's been controlling everything for centuries, and we were little more than her puppets."

The conversation was cut short as the golden-headed Taraghlan came into view, his arm wrapped around the shoulders of a petite girl with flowing coffee-coloured hair. Her green eyes stared venomously into the faces of the small group, her jaw twitching. As they came closer, Taraghlan gave a nod towards Conner and Erin with a grin. "This is my Jenny. We're all set."

Breaking away from his hold, Jenny narrowed her eyes, holding her hand up to indicate she had something to say. "Not just yet." Putting her hands on her hips, she strode across the clearing and put herself squarely under Erin's nose. "So, you're the one who caused all of this devastation, huh? The devastation that destroyed my home, and killed my parents? You don't look like much."

Erin gazed down at the girl, the snappy retort ready on her lips dying away as her face softened. The memory of Conner's mother was pushed aside as her heart swelled with emotion for the girl before her, shaking with anger. Giving a relenting nod, she replied, "Yes, I am. And I can never undo what has been done, but I'm trying to repair it. You see—"

"Yeah, yeah, I know all about your 'other' personalities," Jenny interrupted, making quotation marks in the air with her fingers. "But I hope you understand that means I still don't feel like I can trust you yet. I'm putting a lot of trust in Taraghlan, as it is. I'll go along with this because he swears this will help in restoring humanity, but don't get any ideas about me being a helpful little human for you."

Jenny's rant over, Erin took a step back, the air knocked from her lungs. *It's never going to leave me, is it? The shame of what happened, or what I did. It'll follow me everywhere.* Not lifting her eyes from the ground, she croaked, "I understand, Jenny. We won't ask you to do anything you don't want. I'm just grateful to have a chance at returning humanity to its rightful place." As Jenny grunted in reply, easing herself back into Taraghlan's arms—who was grinning awkwardly at his mate's rant—Erin glanced over at Conner and asked, "So, where are we heading? We can't sit out here all night."

Pushing himself up off the ground, Conner brushed the loose grass from his rumpled jeans and jerked his head over away from the castle and the smoking town beyond. "Over this way. There's an old war bunker out that way that's *hopefully* been left alone by the roaming werewolves. We can stay there for the night in safety and plot out where we're going. There should be a few supplies too, those old places were packed out to withstand a few decades of war."

Matthew's stomach gave a rumble in response, and he grunted as he lifted himself off the grass. "We better get moving then. Or I'm going to gnaw my own arm off." At the glares from Demitri and Jenny, he gave a wince, shaking his head at himself. "Sorry, I didn't think. But I am hungry."

Erin chuckled at him, slapping a hand against his shoulder as she breezed past, Conner joining her side to fall into step with her, linking their hands. The others all moved forwards with them—except Lucius. As though he could feel the unspoken question from behind his back, Conner halted and turned around slowly, staring back at his father's black gaze. Releasing his grip from Erin's hand and marching back over the clearing, he called out, "What's wrong now, old man? Tired already?"

Lucius gave a snarl, his fangs sliding out as he narrowed his eyes at his son. Conner's frame tensed up at the strange reaction, his right hand sliding from his pocket to grasp the hilt of his sword. Jabbing a finger at his son, Lucius growled, "So, you were going to kill your mother? And now you're planning to do it again, between you and Erin? I can't allow that to happen."

Conner tilted his head, an ear-splitting ring careening from the sword as he drew it from the sheath. "Why should you care? You haven't spoken to one

9

another for centuries. And you fucked off and left her on her own in the village—use whatever excuse you like, but I know you had plenty of women over the years."

"All to forget your mother, boy, nothing else. None of them ever came close to her—and I only left at her request, not because I wanted to. And as for speaking to one another…we speak more often than you might think." Lucius chuckled, a dark sound that made the woods feel colder, and the clouds in the far south feel threatening. He smiled sadistically at Conner's slow, icy stare. "Oh yes. That's right. I knew all about the jewel. I knew all about her cursing you. And yes, I let it all happen. This is bigger than you think, *son*."

"No! Conner, don't!"

Erin's cry came too late, as Conner flew for Lucius' throat with his claws outstretched, an animalistic cry leaving his mouth as he arched his arm. Lucius stepped back, but not in time. Conner's claws scraped over the front of his neck, blood spraying across the moist grass, scarlet glaze on the clean sheet of the forest.

Lucius grasped his throat, fixing Conner with a reflection of his burning amber eyes, sickening sucking and wheezing noises coming from the gaps between his splayed fingers. Blood poured from between them in a torrent, dripping down the front of his shirt. Conner had clearly hit his windpipe and severed it apart with one sweep. Lucius looked up at his eldest son, his eyes full of dirt, blood, and rage. And laughed out loud.

"Why? I know it's a cliché question, but *why?*" Conner hissed at Lucius, clenching his clawed fists.

Lucius grinned lopsidedly, and hobbled, wavering on his legs. He shrugged, scarlet pooling over into his hand as he leaned his spare arm against a tree, leaving a bloodied handprint, a permanent reminder of betrayal. "Why not? There were only two things I have ever wanted to do in my life—destroy humans for what they did, and fuck your mother. I'd do anything she asked of me." He leered at Conner.

Conner swallowed, his throat bobbing, and reached confidently for his sword. "Well," he snarled, "you can serve her in Hell then, where she's going to end up, can't you?" He raised his sword, the tip resting against the side of Lucius' neck. Conner glared into his father's eyes, fixing him with an icy gaze. Lucius stared back, a grin stretching over his lips. "Goodbye, *father*."

The scene before the others unfolded almost in slow motion, as though they were not really watching it in front of them, but far away. There was a soft snick of the blade as it cut through flesh, and then a deathly silence. Even the lone bird silenced its calls, and the wind dropped, as though holding its breath. The trees stood still, gravely contemplating what had happened before them. Lucius blinked for a second, a final goodbye to the world he had hated for so long, and a gurgling noise echoed through him. It started at his throat and continued through his body, the only noise the others could hear. As his eyes slid closed, his head glided from his shoulders, bumping onto the ground softly and rolling away along the grass. It picked up speed as it disappeared over the rise of the hill, flailing sinew and liquid as it sped away. Conner's sword fell by his side, clanging against the metal fastening of his boots, echoing in the forest around them.

Erin strode over towards him, spinning him to face her and wrapping her arms around his torso, embracing him silently. His hands came up to rest in her hair, absent-mindedly stroking it as he gazed blankly over her head. "What have I done?" he croaked.

"Sh. If it wasn't you, it would have been me," Erin

whispered, glancing up and running her fingers along his cheek. "Lucius was evil. There's nothing else to it. And he said he wouldn't have let us do what needed to be done. Think of the humans. Think of the millions we're going to save. Don't waste your thoughts on him." She raised pale blue eyes, her heart bursting in her chest for the emotion she saw well up in his eyes.

He shook his head, a bitter expression casting a cloud over his features. "I know, I'm going to. But if I had only done that years ago—"

"Hey, no. None of that," Erin gently admonished, tip-toing to press a loving kiss against his firm lips. Her stomach fluttered at the touch out of instinct, but her soul felt too weighed down for it to be anything more than a caring gesture. "We have to look forwards now. The future. The future we're going to save." She broke the hug with a soft smile, glancing around the group. Her face paled as she did a quick count in her head, swallowing back her worry, "Where's Sukema?"

Conner snapped from his reverie, blinking as he followed her line of sight, swearing under his breath. "Fuck! She must have run off when I was dealing with Lucius. She can't have gone far, come on!" He broke into a run, heading back towards the castle, when Taraghlan flew forwards, snatching his arm. Conner jolted back at the hold, glaring disdainfully back at the general. "Let go of me, Taraghlan. You're still on probation, remember?"

"I haven't forgotten," Taraghlan rasped, lowering his voice. "And I'd rather you didn't worry Jenny with that fact. But we can't go chasing after her—the guards will be out soon to find out where we went, and while I think most of us are hardened warriors, I don't feel up to taking on the whole army. Do you?"

Conner glowered down at the blonde-haired

werewolf, taking in the steadiness of his stormy-eyed gaze. He let out a heavy sigh, relaxing his shoulders as he gave a relenting nod. "Fine. You're right, of course. Shit!" He twisted around and slammed his fist into one of the nearby tress. The trunk didn't break except for a few splinters of bark, but it creaked in protest. "We should have been watching her more closely. What do you think she's going to do?"

Matthew ran a hand through his purple-hued hair, shaking his head briskly. "She's going to tell whoever she can, isn't it? We better get moving. Fast."

Sukema watched the events unfold with watchful brown eyes, taking care to note when the others stepped forwards towards Conner and Lucius. Biting her lip against the raw pain searing through her tightly-bound wrists, she fumbled again with the knot, finally wriggling it free. The rope loosened around her arms, and she bent them with a hiss as her nerves stabbed with feeling once again.

They're not looking. Morons. Now's your chance. Run! Without making a sound, she tip-toed backwards to the edge of the clearing, still roving her eyes rapidly from one person to another, before darting behind one of the trees. Rubbing at her wrists as she moved, Sukema sped down the hillside, out of their lines of sight. The grass whispered beneath her aching feet as she skirted the small hill, heading back towards the castle.

Her eyes narrowed as the slow burn of anger reached her belly. *I'm going to make them all pay for this. Erin and Filtiarn should be the Alphas. But they don't want to follow through…I'll find someone who will. And I know just the woman.* She had taken in every word of what they had said about Rosa. She was the last hope for the werewolf clan to be strong and powerful, worshipped by humanity instead of locked away in the shadows like a bad memory. Her feet moved faster as the crest of the hill arrived, and the castle came back into view.

She jumped over rocks and jutting tree roots, her walk melting into a sprint as her heart thumped faster, her arms pistoning as salvation came ever closer. The guards at the front of the castle gate saw her as she ran towards them, and gave one another unsure glances, before striding confidently forwards with their swords raised. Sukema held her hands up as she came towards them, wheezing as she gasped air into her lungs after her hurried descent. "Wait! Don't attack! I'm not a traitor," she called out, nodding towards their swords. They ignored her cry, continuing forwards with their weapons gleaming in the late evening sun. Her eyes widened as they came over to her, and she took a nervous step back. "Please, you have to believe me! You've been tricked, Erin and Filtiarn are not coming back. Conner has come back."

At her words, the two guards paused, lowering their blades as one. The larger of the two guards came forwards, jutting his chin towards her and fixing her with his hard green eyes. "Is what you say the truth?"

"Yes!" she cried out, jabbing a finger back towards the hillside. "They're getting away now —heading for an old war bunker, or something. You have to chase them." Lowering her hands uncertainly, she added, "I am not your enemy. I am *theirs*. Conner is no Alpha of mine."

"Then who do you claim loyalty to?"

Sukema smiled wryly, lifting her chin proudly, a shiver running along her spine as she replied, "I swear loyalty to Clan Athol, the werewolves within this castle,

Rosa Woods, and my Alpha...Filtiarn Woods."

Chapter Two

Matthew pulled up the lid of the antiquated bunker, Demitri leaning over to help him with a harsh grunt. Matthew gazed up with a raised eyebrow at Conner. "Are you sure this bunker is deserted?" he asked, his tone unsure.

Conner nodded, furrowing his brows and leaning over. "Pretty sure. There was no reason for the lycanthropes to go down there. Why?"

"Because it smells like week-old tripe. It stinks as though something is rotting down there."

Conner glanced back up at Matthew, his lips straightening into a firm line. "You're right," he agreed, his hand sliding along to his sword, slowly gripping it with his fingers. "And worse than that, it smells like rotting *werewolves*."

The entire group cast doubtful glances at one another, before Erin cleared her throat. "Well, if they smell like that, then they're unlikely to be wandering around, are they?"

Jenny nodded eagerly, but Taraghlan shook his head slowly at both of them. "Unfortunately not so, ladies. It may very well mean that's the case, but it could also mean they haven't fed for a while. It's not healthy for werewolves to go without eating meat for a while—any meat, before you start to worry, Jenny," he added at her nervous swallow. "And it is probably the second option."

Conner pointed at Matthew and Demitri, then

pointed at the hatch. "We'll have to go down there, either way. You ladies stay up here with Taraghlan. We'll go down and check."

Matthew gagged as he came down the ladder into the bunker's main room. There were drips of foul-smelling liquid echoing around the room, plopping noisily into small puddles of oily waste. A rat squeaked in the corner, wildly diving for cover under a rusty pipe, away from the unwelcome invaders. The lighting was dim and orange, like something from a nightmarish nuclear bunker after the bombs had fallen, the single lamp in the room swaying from the breeze above from the hatch. A spider tried to stay on for dear life, also swaying precariously, before falling off to find a new life elsewhere in the strange universe of dim lighting and death-like scents.

Half of the furniture in the room was either covered with cloths, half-falling away or tipped over, as though a fight had broken out in the room. The light swaying made the shadows on the walls and floor dance menacingly around the small group of three werewolves. The rotten smell of death and unclean things hung around them, sticking to their skin. Conner's stomach gave an unbidden lurch as he scanned the room.

He twirled the sword handle in his fist, making the blade spin and glint in the low light. He nodded towards Demitri and Matthew, indicating for them to follow him closely. They picked their way across the debris of the room, gagging every few seconds as the stench grew worse. The light creaked above them, and Demitri jumped nervously. Conner glanced back at him coldly, and Demitri mouthed '*sorry*' before they continued across the room. *Still, I feel the tension too.* It itched under Conner's skin, prickling and electric.

A sound made him halt sharply. He held up his hand for the other two to stop, and listened intently, cocking his ear to the far side of the room. Across the sounds of the creaking lamp, and the distant whistle of the wind as it blew through the hatch and down the ladder, they could hear something else. Something much more real and warm. A haggard but steady breathing. It was rasping and very alive, a cold, hellish sound ringing across the broken tables. The fear of what it could be was greater than the fear of knowing what it was.

Conner confidently threw his chin up, and spoke in a loud clear voice, "I order you to show yourself!"

There was a weak chuckle from behind one of the chairs, and a reedy, rasping voice replied, "And just who the hell might you be? What a strange person, to be asking anyone to show himself or herself. You don't know who *I* am."

Conner snarled, his eyes melting into mirrors. "I am Conner, Alpha of the werewolves. And I order you once more, to *show* yourself."

The voice chuckled once more, and sighed quietly, a sound of loneliness and grief. "Oh, are you then? I don't care. Werewolves ripped everyone I know apart. And then one of them grabbed me and turned me into this...this...thing!" The voice ended in a sob. "I don't see why I should show myself. I would rather I didn't, and then you could kill me, and we would all feel better. I certainly wouldn't feel so in pain right now."

Demitri and Matthew's faces both softened a little, but Conner remained unmoved. He was used to the trickery of bloodlusting werewolves, and ninety-nine times out of a hundred, it *was* trickery. He shook his head firmly. "Bullshit. Just come out and have a fair fight. By the smell of it down here, you've been feeding well enough to fight me easily."

"Hah!" The voice cried out in retaliation. "Feeding! Yes, I most certainly have been. First, we fed on the ones who died down here, and then we fed on the ones that became too ill to know what was happening. Then we fed on the first one to fall asleep. We didn't really sleep after that." The voice gave a high-pitched, nervous giggle. "Then we waited for sleep to fall on another, and fed on them. Then we began to try to kill each other. There were only two of us left yesterday, and I fed on *him*, so I suggest you leave or I'm probably going to try and feed on you." The voice went quiet, and an almost silent sob could be heard from behind the chair.

Conner frowned, loosening his grip on his sword. To Matthew and Demitri's surprise, he strode boldly over to the chair. He grasped it solidly and threw it out of the way, smashing it against the far wall, a cloud of dust settling across the floor. Behind the chair crouched a small figure. A young boy, no more than twelve or thirteen. His thin arms were wrapped around himself, his tattered clothing falling off in pieces. Even though he was shaking—either from fear, or cold—he bravely looked up at Conner, sticking his small chin out defiantly. His eyes were a rich scarlet of bloodlust. Conner shivered inwardly as he stared at them, recognising the need that the boy must have been holding back as he glared up at him.

The young boy shrugged. "Well? What now? Well done for revealing me, an astounding trick." His eyes fearfully flitted over to the gleaming sword in his persecutor's hand. "Are you going to kill me?" His voice changed as he asked this, becoming weak and shaky.

Conner said nothing for a moment, cold as ice,

staring down at the small figure before him. Demitri and Matthew stared at him silently, as though fearing the worse. Conner sighed, and relaxed his grip on the hilt of the sword. The young boy closed his eyes for a second, as though praying gratefully to whichever god had just prevented his death. Conner gazed back at the boy's eyes with a softer expression and shook his head. "What happened? Were you stuck down here with some other humans? When did this happen to you?"

The boy nodded, rubbing his knees nervously with his hands. "I came down here with my parents. There were about twenty of us all together. They knew about the bunker, it's been here for years. After the battle had stopped, and it all fell quiet, they went up to look for supplies. They never returned." The boy paused for a second, allowing his words to sink in. "There were about ten of us then, all kids or teens. An adult came down one day, and he said he would help us. He said our parents had been killed by the werewolves, and that he and his group were looking for orphaned children. They were going to look after all of them now. 'They' turned out to be werewolves too, but they looked human to us. He said they could take care of us, that they were going to make up for the 'bad' werewolves that killed everyone...and...and he turned us. Him and his group. Then he left, saying we were not to follow, that he would be back in a few days, and that he was going to find food for us. So we waited a few days. Then a few more. Then a few more. Then we realised he wasn't coming back."

Demitri broke in. "You mentioned you had to...to...feed on one another?" Conner gave him a quick sideways look at the understanding tone in his voice. Demitri's forced feeding from Erin when she was under Sioctine's control was still fresh in everyone's minds.

"Yes. We had no choice. We were so hungry. And none of the food helped. For some reason, it didn't seem to fill us up. I remember the man saying that the meat left was nowhere near the quality that we needed to survive. So we ended up killing each other. And now I'm the only one left." The boy ended on another sob, hiding his face in his lap, bringing his knees up to his chest.

Conner held out his hand to the boy, smiling gently. "Come on, son. We'll help you. It's our duty to return the world to what it was. It's not your fault you were brought into all of this."

The boy glanced up, and smiled innocently through his tears, gratefully placing his small hand in Conner's. "Thank you, mister," he whispered.

Matthew stepped forwards anxiously, but Conner stopped him with a gesture. "It's fine, Matthew, don't worry." he said, confidently.

"Yes, Matthew, don't worry," the boy hissed. His eyes took on a strange gleam, and his grip tightened on Conner's hand. "It's all fine," he continued, his small fangs sliding out wickedly.

Before Conner could even blink, the boy attached himself firmly to Conner's wrist, tearing into it with sighs of pleasure. Matthew and Demitri quickly spun around as more small figures leapt out from various hiding places around the room, hissing and laughing. Tinkling children's laughter. The tattered figures raced over to the group of werewolves, their speed faster than sound.

Conner growled and threw the boy off his wrist, slamming him into the far wall. The boy seemed not to notice, wiping up the dribbling blood from his chin, sucking it from his fingers, oblivious to the injuries he could have suffered from been thrown into a brick wall.

The other children leapt onto Demitri and

Matthew, thrown off in all directions as the pair growled and turned, their eyes glinting amber in warning. Conner ran over and stayed Demitri's hand as it went for the knife at his side.

"No!" he cried out. "You mustn't kill them! They don't know what they're doing, it's the bloodlust—they're children, by the gods!"

Demitri nodded, and gestured back towards the hatch. Matthew nodded firmly, and barged at the small sentry of children who were starting to congregate in front of them again. He knocked all of them flying sideways with moaning protests, and Demitri and Conner raced after him. The three of them hurriedly jumped onto the ladder, climbing as fast as they could manage. Conner, who was last, felt a child reaching for his leg and scratching his ankle with its fangs. He shook his leg quickly, hearing a thump on the floor below. He raced up after the others, and sprang out of the hatch, slamming the door shut after him.

The three of them collapsed on the ground, breathing heavily. Erin came over from the patch of grass where she sat with Taraghlan and the two other women, and raised an eyebrow. She took a second to rove her gaze across their rapidly rising and falling chests and clawed garments, letting out a heavy sigh. "I'm guessing it's not so safe then?"

Conner shook his head. "Not as yet, no. But it will be. There are children down there—werewolf children. We just need to find them some meat so they can come out of the bloodlust. Then we can talk to them normally."

Matthew shot up, his face black with anger. "Are you mad? You're going to put us all into danger, because of them? It doesn't matter if they are adults, or children, or cute fluffy little kittens, they are frenzied *werewolves*!

They're not going to listen to reason now."

Conner raised himself up on his elbows, fixing Matthew with an icy stare. "They are children though, Matthew. They didn't choose to be turned, did they? And they never would have been turned if it wasn't for us."

"Us? *Us?*" Matthew jumped up, his vivid eyes flashing. "There were no *us* that started this war! It was you and Erin. *We* were locked in a dungeon, remember?"

Conner shrugged, pushing himself off the ground and clicking his shoulders as he eased feeling back into them. "That's fine, Matthew. You don't have stay with our little group. You're more than welcome to go off on your own."

"What?" Matthew stopped in mid protest, his mouth falling open.

Conner folded his arms across his chest with a stern frown. "Oh, yes. No one has said you have to stick within our little pack, Matthew. But let me tell you this. If you *do* want to stay with us, you had better start remembering who is your Alpha, and you had better start doing as he asks."

Erin broke in, clearing her throat sharply. "Actually, Conner, I think you'll find it's what *she* asks. And at this point, I'm afraid I agree with Matthew. I see little point in saving a few if half of us die. We are needed for a lot more than getting ourselves away."

Conner smiled gently. "I know, darling. Sorry, I...I got a little too used to ruling in your stead." He shoved his hands into his back pockets, nodding over to her. The light fell from his eyes. "And you're right, unfortunately. I know you are. I just didn't want to think it." His voice cracked, and he added, "We must move on quickly, then. This will weigh heavily on me until we can come back for them."

Chapter Three

"So you see, they are going to try the route *you* said they wouldn't, hmm? Sometimes you really ought to listen to your mother."

Filtiarn gave a shrug, rubbing his fingers over his chin. "Oh, well. You were right, I was wrong. They still think I'm dead, though, that's a plus." He leaned forwards over the back of the armchair, clasping his hands together as he grinned back at Rosa. "I don't see what difference it makes if our plan is to return to the castle, anyway."

Rosa smiled cruelly, silhouetted against the tall roaring fire in front of her. They stood in a small drawing room, the only light in the dark room coming from the flickering red and gold of the flames in the fireplace, licking their way up the chimney. A somewhat moth-eaten rug lay beneath the pair of red leather chairs, a vivid Persian pattern snaking across the length of it. The walls were adorned with large portraits of stern men and women. Only one, which was hung above the fireplace, looked different. It showed a portrait of a young Lucius, but he was smiling at the artist, instead of the usual cold, fixed stare. But the smile held no warmth. It was cruel, much like the figure stood in front of the fireplace now. Rosa cleared her throat. The room was one of many in the house Rosa rented, an Elizabethan gatehouse of a manor long since fallen into disrepair. "I just like to keep track of them, that's all. Especially as..." Her voice trailed off, the grin falling from her features, and her hand came up to grip a glass pendant around her neck tightly. "Especially now your father is dead."

Filtiarn's face drained of colour as he gazed back at her, his jaw dropping open. "He's...dead? How can you know?"

Her fingers delved into the top of her dress, pulling out the chain and glass pendant out. A crack ran along its polished surface, tiny imperfections clear in the flickering light from the fire. In a broken voice, she explained, "This was enchanted, so I knew he was okay. If it ever breaks...he has died." Her fingers curled tightly around the glass disc as she turned her face away, blinking back the hot tears that stabbed at her eyes.

There was a scrape against fabric as Filtiarn's claws sliced into the smooth leather, his fangs sliding out on a snarl. "Then Conner shall pay for that as well."

Rosa's tears stilled as she read between the lines of his words, turning back to her son with a hardened gaze. Her skirt rustling as she moved along the wooden floorboards towards him, she narrowed her eyes. "You mean *both of them* shall pay. Not just Erin."

"Of course, mother. I was just thinking out loud," Filtiarn answered breezily, almost too fast. He raised his eyes to Rosa's frown deepened, and she let out a heartfelt sigh, skirting the chair as she sat in it heavily.

Pyramiding her hands under her chin, she fixed him with a deep stare, as if trying to stare into his very soul. It was no secret to her that Filtiarn had always been jealous of his brother's connection to Erin...mostly because he had coveted Erin from afar himself. *And I know he still harbours these silly feelings for her. He better forget about them if he wants this to work.*

She waved her hand over towards a nearby servant, snapping her fingers hurriedly as the smartly-dressed girl came forwards, offering forwards a large glass of red wine on a silver tray. The girl bowed as Rosa lifted the glass into her hand, twisting and casting a sly glance at Filtiarn as she scurried back to the dark corner of the room. He caught her eye and smirked, running a hand through his hair as his silvery eyes followed her movements.

Rosa cleared her throat sharply, dragging his attention back to her. "If you've quite finished eyeing up the staff, Filtiarn?"

"Sorry, mother." He gave a chuckle, but the flirtation has the effect of calming him down, his claws and fangs receding into his body as quickly as they had appeared. He jerked his head towards her, straightening his spine with a soft click. "So where do I need to go?"

Taking a long sip of her wine, Rosa leaned her head back against the chair, grinning to herself as she gazed into the flames. The rich warmth of the alcohol spread down her throat, matching the heat blooming in her cheeks from the fire. Swallowing the wine back, she answered, "I need you to follow them while I go to the castle. Don't worry about me—I have the situation under control. But I need someone to make sure they come back."

A dark expression ghosted over Filtiarn's features, making his sensual smirk look almost maniacal in the dim light. "I think I can manage that. It'll be fun."

Chapter Four

The group gathered around a small house, the building next door shattered in half. It was caved in on one side, showing the rooms of both upstairs and downstairs, like the skeleton of the house. A single bed hung off the edge of what was once a young boy's bedroom, creaking forlornly in the wind, a football poster flapping busily around one of the legs.

But the house that Erin and the others assembled around in tight formation was still in one piece, despite looking worse for wear, paint peeling from the windows, themselves smashed in places. There were distant noises from within the building, as though people were talking. Erin silently nodded at Conner, who bent his head in response, motioning over his shoulder for Taraghlan to come up close behind him, along with Jenny. Erin had Matthew and Demitri close behind. They were taking no chances of being taken by surprise this time.

Gently, Conner pushed the red front door open, his eyes narrowing in suspicion as it swung open easily. Erin moved across to the doorway, her feet making no noise on the dusty pavement, and glanced inside. She saw nothing but a bare room, the walls torn free of paper, covered in graffiti. A couple of cardboard boxes were in the corner, one of them hastily covered with a dirty white tablecloth. The room looked like a squatter's hideout — until Erin spotted the tell-tale signs of what they were looking for.

Blood. Smeared across one of the walls, streaking across like a banner, a single handprint visible at the end of it. The smell hit next, a sickening twist of sweetness and death.

Erin swallowed, moving back nervously. Her stomach lurched at the scent, but her lycanthrope instincts kicked in at the fragrance, making her mouth well with saliva. None of them had eaten yet, all supplies nowhere to be found in the apocalyptic wasteland left from the battles. Conner glanced over at her with a raised eyebrow, but she nodded and gave a tight smile. Moving like a shadow, Conner crouched down, and crept into the bare house. The sounds of someone talking came through from the next room, but if was muffled and subdued. Conner motioned towards the others, who silently followed him into the room, those with weapons gripping them tightly.

Conner sniffed and leaned back towards Erin and Taraghlan. "There are only two of them in there, I can't smell any others. I think we should just go in."

They both nodded at him firmly, and he moved forwards. He jutted his chin up proudly, and called out loudly. "I am Conner, Alpha werewolf. Show yourselves. This building has been claimed."

The talking abruptly stopped, and whispers could be heard, sounding rushed and strained. There was a bump from the next room, then silence again. Eventually, a tearful face appeared around the side of the doorframe between the two rooms. It belonged to a young girl, pale and thin. Her eyes were deep silver, drained of any emotion, filled only with longing and hunger. Her hand appeared below her face, stained with blood from many days before, the fingernails broken and dirty, gripping the doorframe with a desperate clinch. When she spoke, her voice was a hollow, hoarse sound. "I don't know who you are, or what you mean, but it doesn't matter. You have to go, you're in danger."

The face began to disappear again around the side of the frame, but Erin quickly spoke up, halting the young girl. "Wait! We know what you are. We're werewolves too. We're here to help you."

The girl shook her head forlornly. "If you know what we are, then you really are stupid. We've been feeding off anything and everyone who moved within a mile of here. We just fed, which is the only reason you are not being attacked right now. The pain never goes away..." The young girl trailed off, licking her lips.

Erin shook her head firmly. "Listen to me. We are not afraid of you. A plan is in motion to save yourselves and others like you—as well as take down the creatures that first created you."

There was a long pause as the girl continued casting her eyes over Erin's figure, furrowing her brow as though an unspoken question was forming in her mind. Recognition flashed into her glassy irises, and she let out a sharp gasp. "Hang on, I recognise you! Y-You're the one from the TV! You and him!" Her trembling finger jabbed out towards Conner, who hung his head shamefully at her accusation. Erin glanced over her shoulder at him, casting her eyes to the floor as she turned back to the young girl. The girl's finger dropped as she fixed her glare on Erin, adding, "*You* were the ones who started all this in the first place." Her blood-stained fangs slid out from under her upper lip, her hand gripping the doorframe determinedly, despite shaking with fear.

Erin nodded and hung her head slightly, taking the anger directed towards her with a heavy heart. When she next spoke, her voice resonated with solemnity. "I know that. And you don't know how sorry I am. But this is why we're trying to make it right again. We are going to try and help every life we destroyed."

"Oh? And how do we know that you are going to stick to that? How do we know you are not just another group of bastards like the ones that did *this* to us?"

Taraghlan opened his mouth to speak, but Erin held her palm up to him, a commanding signal not to speak. As he closed his mouth again in subdued acknowledgement, Erin gave a harsh sigh. "You don't. But you have two choices. You either stay like this, furrowing out a living until you end up killing each other and losing all your humanity, or you take a chance and come with us. A chance is better than no chance at all, at least?"

The girl glared back at Erin for a moment, as though the words were sinking in. "Give me a moment," she whispered, vanishing from view back around the corner. There was more muttering from around the corner in the next room, and the girl reappeared, this time fully in view. A small child was by her side, with the same hungry silver eyes. The older girl protectively put an arm around the small girl's shoulders, and pulled her swiftly next to her. She cleared her throat. "This is my younger sister, Amber," she explained. "And my name is Florence — well, I'm called Flo most of the time."

Erin held her hand out in welcome, a smile twitching at the corners of her mouth. "I am Erin. Are there any more of you?"

Flo shook her head. "No, it's just us. Our parents were killed the first day of the attacks."

Jenny flinched, but only Taraghlan noticed. He wrapped an arm tightly around her waist, stroking a thumb across her cheek. She relaxed in his hold, sinking against him as she looked down to the floor.

Erin motioned for the two girls to follow the

group, turning to leave the house. There was another moment of hesitancy from the older girl before she relented, following in trepidation She kept a wary eye on the group, gripping her young sister's hand tightly. As the small procession strode out of the front door into the street, Conner tapped Erin on the back, pulling her back from the others as he captured her lips in a quick kiss. "Well done, darling. Truly done like a Queen."

Erin grinned, her face glowing at Conner's comment, but it soon disappeared, and her eyes grew dark again as she turned her attention to the task before them as she followed the others into the dilapidated street. The two girls stood nervously at the edge of the group, waiting for what would be next. Flo spoke up, her voice croaky in the dusty air. "Well, what are we going to do for food? We've been feeding, but none of it seems to be enough. A few meals here and there," she paused as she noticed the uneasy look on Jenny's face, "but both of us are still constantly hungry. I don't know how you plan to counteract that."

Erin gazed across at Conner with a shrug, who simply replied, "Don't worry, we can get you food. You just have to trust us—you won't hurt us, honestly. You're not that far gone yet, believe me."

The little girl surprised everyone with her sweet, childish voice, gazing around at them as though she was comfortable being in the middle of a destroyed street with adult werewolves. "Are you going to stop my tummy hurting? I don't like it. I don't want to keep eating the funny meat that Flo gives me."

Flo gazed down at the floor for a second, before her silver-glazed eyes rose up again and met with the group. She placed her hands over her young sister's ears, and then whispered, "Look, I...I had to get it from somewhere. There were other teenagers. I hated doing it. But I've been telling her it was just meat I scavenged, to get her to eat it. Please don't tell her anything different, I don't want her to know." The pain in her eyes was evident as she released her hold from her young sister's ears. She glanced away again, hanging her hands by her sides. The little girl looked up briefly, eyeing her older sister with curiosity, before looking back at Erin with a soft smile.

Erin crouched down, smiling at the small girl, gazing into her moon-coloured irises. "Amber, I promise you we will stop your tummy hurting. But we have to go on a long walk, and you must be very brave, and do everything your big sister tells you do to. Can you do that?"

Amber nodded slowly, the gravity of the situation furrowing her young brow. She gripped Flo's hand tightly, pulling herself further back. Flo squeezed her young sister's hand in return, moving her behind her arm.

Erin rose up again, meeting Taraghlan's eyes as she did so. He was watching her with a strange curiosity, as if he had never seen anyone show such a caring, thoughtful attitude towards a child before. Erin briefly wondered what his own upbringing had been like, if that was what had honed him into such a cold, hard person.

The group made their way off towards the distant woods, the only place where the word 'safety' could be waveringly used. The world behind them—the skeleton houses, and the floating remnants of life eerily lit against the dark setting sun—disappeared from view, as though from a distant nightmare.

Chapter Five

araghlan sat down next to the edge of the small camp, where Erin sat hugging her knees, staring into the thick darkness of the forest. He gave a quick glance at her, staring wistfully into the distance, unblinking. "You were always a little more human than the rest of us, you know."

Erin blinked up at Taraghlan's stony face, raising her eyebrow delicately. "What do you mean?"

Taraghlan gazed up into the night sky, his eyes following the steady passage of clouds across the pale moon. "You never had quite the killer instinct we did — which was good, don't get me wrong. Too much bloodshed, and we kill ourselves. But you do understand why that is, don't you?"

Erin rolled her eyes, and took a heavy breath in. "Why does everyone keep expecting me to remember things all the time? I barely remember the scraps I have recovered. It's like seeing scenes from a film, but I can't remember the name of the film. I'm not even sure that they happened to me at all sometimes, or if I've just been told so, and brainwashed. I don't know anything about the world that I'm in at the moment. I know I said back at the castle that more and more was tumbling into place...but we are talking about two-thousand years' worth of memories, not what the face of that guy you met at a party was called."

Taraghlan ran his hand across from his sword hilt

to the grass below, stroking his hand across the fresh blades of grass, erupting in scent in the already sweet air of the cool night. "Okay, well, I think you should know something. There is a reason that you were different from most of us—and so was Conner until…" Taraghlan paused, spinning his forefinger next to his head in a '*crazy*' motion. "But those of us who came later, including myself, were….a little different."

"In what way?"

"We….are not all pure werewolves like yourself and Conner. We are more like hybrids."

Erin's eyebrows shot upwards, her interest piqued. "In what way? Hybrids with what?"

Taraghlan's eyes cooled, even icier than they had been before. "After you left the village, thanks to Filtiarn's doing, Rosa took over the pack—as you already know. But what you don't know is how she twisted things. She uses magic, you know. Wields it as deftly as any witch."

Erin turned over so she was leaning on her side, listening intently as her heartbeat picked up in response to the tension held in his voice. The soft night air drifted some of her hair over her face, and she brushed it away with a casual motion. "I think you better tell me what happened."

Taraghlan nodded slowly, more to himself than Erin. When he next spoke, his voice was soft and whispery. "Well, she knew that the werewolves would never fully agree to her being Alpha—she always stated that she was simply 'holding your place' until you returned. But she needed wolves on her side, so Rosa turned to magic. The only way werewolves could be created at that point was through the gods or the…er…*usual* channels, if you catch my drift. But somehow she created werewolves from willing humans, using spells and rituals. Those created werewolves saw her as Alpha, but as a product of their creation, they were more bloodthirsty than their pure counterparts. I, along with many others, am the results of this. My father was a pure werewolf, but my mother was a created werewolf."

Erin leaned her head to the side in surprise, her eyes widening. "Shit. Rosa really did go on a little power trip, huh? I suppose it explains the old myths and stories of becoming a werewolf." Erin paused and gave Taraghlan a wry grin. "I guess it explains some of the...colder behaviour you exhibit."

A chill wind picked up and whistled past, blowing the leaves of the ancient oaks behind them. As the wind died, the night air grew quieter, the moon sliding behind a wispy grey cloud, taking a sly peep from behind it. Taraghlan's hair loosed itself in the cold air, drifting behind him in a curtain of gold. With calm features, he grabbed it and tucked it back again before turning to shrug at Erin. His features were relaxed, but she noticed his jaw twitching as he ground his teeth, his grey eyes burning almost to black with quiet fury. "I think I'll have to cut it off. It's more fashionable this century anyway." He flicked it back over his shoulder, linking his hands together before fixing Erin with a penetrating stare. "My upbringing has more to do with that than my heritage does."

"Oh?"

The hand brushed over the gleaming hilt of the sword again, but quicker, almost nervously. "My mother was heartless. My father died when I was very young, so I don't remember a lot about him. My mother brought me up. But she hated me. She had only gone with my father as it seemed to be the only choice for the created lycanthropes at that point. She despised pure werewolves, and she always said she saw half of my father in me. I think she hoped I would have more...fury in me than I did. At any rate...she wasn't exactly what I would expect a mother to be, put it that way. I soon learned that in life you either lie down and get spat on, or you stand up and do the spitting. I became strong through struggle. That's why I'm cold."

Erin let out a low breath. "I'm starting to think there's no one here who had a normal upbringing?"

Taraghlan smiled ruefully. "We'd be human if we had. With the exception of Jenny, and her life has taken a turn for the strange."

Footsteps came up behind them, striding purposefully through the undergrowth of the forest floor. Matthew emerged, holding two limp rabbits in his hands. He lifted them in a gesture to Erin and Taraghlan. "I've got the food for everyone. Sorry it's not more, but it's all I could find. I'm going to give some to the girls first. Are they still waiting?"

Erin nodded, jumping up from the damp grass. Her shoulders stiffened as she thought once more of the young girls waiting on the other side of the camp, two more casualties of the war. "Yes, I'll walk over with you." She nodded towards Taraghlan, who leaned back onto the grassy bank with a contented sigh. "We'll talk more later, Taraghlan." He gave a mock salute and continued to look into the distance, as if he were simply a human man with all the time in the world.

Erin raised her eyebrows at Matthew, who shrugged gently in return. Erin turned towards the two girls waiting in the forest clearing under the watchful eye of Demitri. The sisters sat in front of the crackling fire, orange sparks snapping and leaping for freedom, the long flames licking up towards the dark, velvety night sky.

They stared into the heart of the fire, their eyes no longer silver, but burnt orange from the colours reflected into them. Amber was tucked tightly into Flo, Flo's arm wrapped around her little sister. Amber absent-mindedly sucked her thumb, while Flo's face was still, the cogwheels of her mind spinning in fury.

Matthew strode over towards them as he handed the larger of the two rabbits to Erin, tearing into the other one with his claws. Pulling chunks of torn pink flesh free, he held them out towards Flo. "Here you are, girls. Some food for you."

Amber glanced up sleepily, still sucking her thumb. She screwed her nose up in disgust, sticking her tongue out. "Flo, I don't want that meat again! I don't like it!"

Flo immediately put a finger towards her lips in a shushing motion, looking around nervously. "Amber, please stop shouting. We *need* to be quiet. Okay?"

Amber looked up sharply at Flo's face, her bottom lip wavering. "But I don't *want* it," she protested with a whine.

Matthew knelt down so he was level with Amber's small, if somewhat dirty, face. He glanced at Flo, placing his hand on her knee in a fatherly motion. "Don't worry," he smiled, "I'll help."

He turned to Amber again with a forced grin, and pointed at the slab of meat. "You don't like the taste of these?" Amber shook her head determinedly, still scowling at the flesh. "Tell you what. You eat this, and I'll find you whatever else you really want to eat. Deal?"

Amber's eyes widened at the thought. "Chocolate," she replied, licking her lips eagerly

"No problem—chocolate. I promise we'll find you some," Matthew continued, holding the meat out in offering. "*If* you eat this now. Can you do that for me?"

Amber gave the meal a doubtful glance, before nodding silently and taking it from his outstretched hand, digging in as though she hadn't eaten for some time. Flo looked up with a shocked expression at Matthew as she took some of the meat from him. "Thank you," she mumbled shyly.

Erin appeared around the lines of trees, smiling over at the two girls as she watched them eagerly swallow down the rabbit. She took a deep breath in, closing her eyes at the sweet, clean scent of the night air. Matthew gingerly sat down near the fire, folding his legs in a swift movement. Erin's eyes scanned the area as she took in the trees, the deep green ivy crawling over the ancient trunks, and narrowed her eyes. "Where are Conner and the others? I left them here with the girls."

Flo looked up from her meal, wiping the side of her mouth swiftly with the back of her thin hand. "I know where they went," she interjected.

"Where?"

Flo pointed off into the darkness. "There was a weird noise, they went off to investigate it. Demitri was here, but he said that Jenny would be okay watching us, didn't he?" Flo glanced over at Jenny, who nodded to confirm. "Then you and Matthew came by."

"Thank you, Flo." Erin made her way through the legs of the group, Sioctine gleaming wickedly by her side. She looked down at Matthew, her lips in a firm line. Worry gnawed at her gut, a deep hole that grew darker by the second. *Why would Conner and the others just run off like that? It's not safe. Something doesn't add up here.* "Matthew, can you stay here with the girls? I'm going to try and find the others—we should be staying together, not wandering off into the woods whenever we fancy."

Matthew nodded and gazed towards the two young werewolves. "Of course, Erin, we'll be fine here. Won't we, girls?"

As Erin strode purposefully off into the woods, her figure swallowed up quickly by the dark trunks of the trees and shadows that danced wildly about the fire, Flo watched her walk off with a strange look in her silver eyes. A grin turned the corners of her mouth, and her fangs slid out in menace.

Chapter Six

Rosa strode through the main passage as though she had lived in the castle for years. Her eyes cast upwards, she took in the sight of the long banners and tapestries. *Hmm...I suppose they can stay. After all, we need to at least **pretend** Erin is coming back.* Her ring-encrusted fingers trailed along the threads of the fabric, tracing lines of the dancing figures and wolves. A few of the guards stepped aside as she careered through, nodding respectfully at her. Clearly, they still understood Filtiarn as being in charge—not Conner. A smile curled her painted lips.

She rounded the corner into her private quarters. It hadn't been difficult getting the room. She had proclaimed Filtiarn had been called away for something important, and that she would simply stay in the castle quietly and not interfere. Rosa bit back a snort. Interfering was exactly what she would be doing. The quarters were simply yet elegantly furnished, as was the rest of the castle. Antique furniture and crisp, clean white sheets on the bed, all graced by the many portraits of the Athol family glaring down at her. She resisted the urge to throw them all into the fire and wipe the smirks from their self-righteous faces, but she contented herself with pouring a large wine instead.

She spun around, her dress rustling as she knocked back a large swallow of the liquid, pausing to retrace her steps to the door and shove it closed. After a second of thought, she reached down to shut the lock close. She didn't need people around for what she was going to prepare. Swallowing the rest of the burgundy, Rosa clanged the glass down onto a nearby table and strode over to the fire, latching her fingers and clicking them back. *Time to get to work.*

She reached for the pendant hanging around her neck, the crack still jaggedly snaking its way through the centre, and yanked it from her neck with a harsh grip. Her face softened as she looked down at it, something aching hard in her chest. *Whatever anyone thought of my decision...I loved Lucius. That's why I told him to go. I didn't want them to kill him.* Her grip tightened, the edges of the glass cutting into her fingers. *And they killed him anyway. Once this was all over, we were going to be together again. Why the hell did he have to let his temper get in the way?*

Pushing back the sting of tears, Rosa gave a loud sniff, placing it down onto the marble hearth. She raised her foot, the ache throbbing in her chest, and slammed her foot down onto it. It broke on contact into tiny slivers, screeching as they slid against the hard surface beneath. A few more stamps, and the pendant was nothing more than a handful of glittering dust. A grunt escaped her lips as she crouched down to scoop it up, settling herself back onto the thickly-fibred rug below. Closing her eyelids, she raised the glass pieces to her mouth, whispering in ancient Irish. *At least his spirit will live on in my spell. The most powerful spell I can cast.* Rosa snapped her eyes open, gazing deeply into the dancing flames of the fire. The heat made redness bloom on her cheeks, and she tried to ignore the uncomfortable heat travelling down her back against the satin of her dress. With a sharp breath, she blew the twinkling shards into the fire.

Nothing happened for a moment, and she

continued concentrating on the flames, willing them to bend to her will. The orange glow disappeared, and burst into green flames. They twisted around one another, wrapping themselves in shades of the forest and ivy. The smile curled Rosa's lips once more, her heart lightening at the sight. *As light as my black heart can feel, anyway.* It was simple now. Within a matter of hours, the werewolves within the castle would do as she asked. The spell didn't exactly turn them into thralls of hers...but the effect was the same.

A loud knock came at the door, startling her from her daydreaming. Swiping her hands hurriedly across the flames to mask them back to orange, she cleared her throat, calling loudly, "One moment. I'll unlock the door."

As the locks clunked back and the door swung wide open, Rosa felt her nerves prickles with tension as she found herself staring into the dark eyes of a young African werewolf. Her curly hair was matted together, as though she hadn't washed for some time, and there were marks and dark circles beneath her eyelids. Jutting her chin proudly, Rosa kept her face straight as she asked, "Yes? Can I help you with something?" *It's strange...she looks familiar, but I can't place her.*

"You certainly can. I'm here to..." The woman leaned in, lowering her voice after checking left and right for anyone listening in. "I'm here to talk about Conner and Erin."

Well...I wasn't expecting that. Rosa restrained herself from showing any reaction to the woman's statement, instead gracefully stepping aside and waving her hand towards the room. "I think you had better come in, er...what did you say your name was?"

"Sukema."

"That's where I know you from," Rosa remarked

out loud, narrowing her eyes. "You were with the traitors, back at Forest Hall. I heard some of the guards mention it." *And I saw it in my mirrors.* She pushed the door closed behind them, leaning against it as she clicked the locks over. The woman before her stared back with wide eyes, a slow swallow passing down her throat as Rosa looked her over, cold suspicion clear in her gaze.

"Yes, but it was all part of Filtiarn's plan. He was the one who told me to pretend to be their friend, to get close to Erin so he could get her back." Sukema wrung her hands together as she stared back at the silent werewolf glaring back at her.

She's telling the truth. I can sense it. Pushing herself away from the door, Rosa strode over and placed her arm around Sukema's shoulders, guiding her over to one of the chairs. Forcing a kind smile on her face, she seated Sukema firmly, straightening herself. Smoothing creases out of her skirt, she swept over the room to pour two more glasses of wine, calling over her shoulder, "I believe you, don't worry. But there's something you should know. Is red okay for you?"

Sukema's dark eyes roved across the bottle in Rosa's hands before she nodded and mumbled, "Yes, thank you. Red is fine. What is it I need to know?"

Rosa gave a chuckle, spinning around with the two glasses, the burgundy within gleaming with red tones in the gentle firelight. Passing one drink over, she took a deep breath. "It was Conner who told you to do all of that, suffering from an illness, of a kind."

"I know that. We all knew that. But it was still Filtiarn, in his mind. The real Filtiarn is long gone."

"No, he's alive." The smile grew wider as Rosa watched the shock spread over Sukema's expression, and her pulse thumped faster as she let the excitement of her words fill her. No one else had known but her —until now. "He's been alive all along. And now he is returning to lead our pack." She took a sip of the rich liquid in her hand, watching Sukema as she dropped to her knees before her.

Sukema grinned wickedly, revealing straight, even teeth. "My Queen Mother, I come to pledge my allegiance to you and your son, to aid you as much as possible in capturing Erin and Conner."

"Oh? In what way?"

"I know where they are headed. There's an old —"

"An old war bunker. Yes, I know already," Rosa sighed, placing her glass down on the polished marble fireplace. The smile faded, and she glared down at Sukema, her gaze hardening. "Here's my problem, Sukema. How do I know you can be trusted?"

Sukema scrambled to her feet, her almond-shaped face paling as she shook her head in confusion, shrugging. "I don't understand. I've told you where they are going, I have sworn my allegiance. You can trust me completely."

Rosa felt tension travel along her nerves again, crackling as she shook her head slowly. "No, Sukema, I can't. You see, you had to also swear allegiance to Conner, or he wouldn't have allowed you into their small pack. However, you have shown that they couldn't trust you." A pang of sadistic triumph worked its way along her spine as she saw a bead of sweat forming on Sukema's brow. She smiled again. *She knows where I'm going with this.*

Faltering, Sukema stammered, "No, no, you don't understand! I didn't want to swear allegiance to him, I only did it for Filtiarn's plan!"

"How do I know you're not tricking me?" Rosa hissed, reaching to the side of the fireplace and pulling a long golden-threaded cord. A bell rang somewhere in the distance as she clasped her hands together, pursing her lips. "I'm afraid you cannot be trusted, *Sukema*. I get the feeling that you simply like to be on the winning side. And as you are unable to tell me anything I cannot find out for myself, you are of no further use to me." A noise came from outside, then a firm knock on the mahogany door. She waved her hands towards the door, releasing the lock with a spiral of magic, and it swung open to reveal two large, towering guards. Jabbing a finger towards Sukema, she commanded, "This is one of the traitors. I want her to be taken to the prisons...and executed."

"What? No! NO! I am on your side! I AM ON YOUR SIDE!" Sukema screamed as the two guards grabbed her under the arms, dragging her from the room. Her coffee eyes were filled with panic as she clawed the furniture and door, desperately clinging on as she cried out, "Please! I'm not a traitor!"

Rosa moved across the room in a sweep of satin as the female werewolf's cries echoed down the corridor, growing fainter as she was taken down to the castle dungeons. Rosa scoffed at the woman's impudence. *To march in here and expect me to take her into the fold. There is only room for Filtiarn and my son, no one else. I don't doubt she would have been loyal to me. But I don't like having loose ends.*

Chapter Seven

"Help!"

The cry made the men snap into awareness. Conner sat opposite the two girls, drifting off into a half-doze, dreaming of better days. He leapt up, still in a strange half-dreaming state, his hand automatically going for the hilt of his sword. Jenny was asleep on the grassy bank, snoring gently. As the scream sounded into the night, she woke up with wide eyes, her breath coming in short bursts as her heartbeat pounded in her ears. *What now?*

Demitri was already up, walking around the small group as he kept watch. He looked off into the shrouding darkness of the woods, his large, outstretched claws gleaming against the shy beams of moonlight filtering through the canopy of trees above. Flo and Amber's faces paled as the cry rang out, Amber clinging to her older sister, sobbing silently into her t-shirt. Flo shushed her, stroking her hair, but her light eyes were wide with fear.

Conner ran over to Demitri. "What the hell was that?" he said in hushed tones. He glanced across to the two young girls with a reassuring grin, but his tone was urgent.

Demitri shook his head, a grim expression crossing his face. "I don't know. Where are Erin and Matthew?"

Conner's eyes opened wider, gleaming with colours that reflected the fire. "They were with Taraghlan.

We have to go and look. He should still be over the other side of the camp."

Demitri nodded, glancing back at the girls. "What about them?" he asked, gesturing.

Conner peered back in the direction of Matthew's thumb. He gazed over at Jenny, holding his breath as he hesitated for a moment. "You stay here with them, look after Jenny and the girls. I'll go and find out where they are." Another scream rang out into the night, piercing the stillness once more. Conner grabbed his sword with a swift motion, jumping to his feet. "I'll be back soon, don't move." Demitri nodded as Conner retreated into the thicket of trees, disappearing into the enveloping darkness.

Demitri stared after him, tapping his foot in a worried staccato. His hand played nervously with the hilt of his knife, turning it over a few times before slowly placing it back into the sheath hanging by his side. He glanced back over at the girls. Amber was still clinging to her older sister, who was gently rocking back and forth. Jenny was bolt upright, clutching her knees to her chin, staring into the comforting flames licking away noisily at the logs beneath.

Demitri nodded over towards them, trying to smile reassuringly. "Don't worry. It won't be anything, Taraghlan will have said something to piss Erin off, that's all." His words were strong, but his voice wavered as he spoke.

Jenny nodded at him, only really half-listening. "I hope so," she whispered, almost to herself.

Another cry rang out from the dark, followed by a loud shout; a strange, strangled cry. Demitri leapt up and raced to the edge of the clearing, his eyes rapidly scanning the darkness, sweat forming on his brow. His hand once again fell to his side, searching for the cool metal of the knife.

"You had better go and look, they might need help."

Demitri peered over his shoulder back at Flo, who had spoken up in a quiet, wobbling voice. Flo glanced over at Jenny, then back at Demitri. "Go on, we'll be fine. Jenny is here as well."

Swallowing hard, Demitri gazed over at Jenny. "I don't know," he said doubtfully.

Jenny looked up at him. "Go on, we'll be okay, Matthew. We'll hide if anyone comes by. You need to help the others. I want them to come back. It's no good us all sitting here and wondering—you heard Erin, we have to stick together."

Demitri bit his lip, clearly torn as to what to do. He paused for a split second before nodding firmly. "Alright. I'll just go and look. That's all. Promise me you will stay here, and you will hide immediately if anyone comes by."

Jenny nodded in return, fisting her hands so tightly that her nails dug into the palms. "Promise." She forced her heartbeat to slow its pace, its rapid throb painful against her temples.

Demitri took a deep breath, scanning one last quick look over the girls, and silently paced off into the trees, his footsteps making almost no sound. Jenny hugged her knees to her chin again, and smiled over at Flo and Amber. "It'll be okay, you know." She met Flo's eyes, but Flo glanced away quickly. Frowning, Jenny craned her neck to see the girls' faces, but they were hidden from her in the half-shadows.

There was a scuffle in the nearby trees as Erin and Matthew pushed through, Matthew holding out two large and strong-smelling rabbits in his enclosed fist. He ripped some chunks out and offered them to the two young girls, mumbling something about food. Amber's defiant childish cry rang through the air as she declared, "Flo, I don't want that meat again! I don't like it!"

Jenny turned her head away, the smell turning her stomach. *How the hell am I going to get used to being around this sort of thing? I imagine Taraghlan tucks into it just as happily.* She tried to focus on the scent of the flowers growing around the base of the tree trunks instead, running her fingers through the delicate stalks as she leaned over to relish the fragrance.

"Where are Conner and the others? I left them here with the girls."

Jenny glanced up sharply as Erin's question pierced her subconscious, and she blinked away the sleep forming in her eyes, looking over towards the female Alpha. She liked Erin, despite the fact she was the one who had caused the war in the first place. *But it wasn't her exactly, it was whatever had a hold of her. Erin herself—the real Erin—is a pretty cool person.* And Jenny felt safe around the group of werewolves, something she hadn't felt for a long time.

Flo glanced up from her meal, wiping the side of her mouth with a single hand, her eyes flashing. "I know where they went," she replied.

"Where?"

Flo jabbed a finger in the direction the others had gone. "There was a weird noise, they went off to investigate it. Demitri was here, but he said that Jenny would be okay watching us, didn't he?" Flo glanced over at Jenny, who nodded to confirm, though something in her stomach twisted in worry. "Then you and Matthew came by."

"Thank you, Flo." Erin paused, gazing off into the woods as her pale hand travelled to the long sword by her side. "Matthew, can you stay here with the girls? I'm going to try and find the others—we should be staying together, not wandering off into the woods whenever we fancy."

"Of course, Erin, we'll be fine here. Won't we, girls?"

Matthew stared after Erin with a dark frown, tapping his fingers impatiently against the side of his jeans as he chewed at his lip. Moments passed, and no one returned from the woods, and no further sound was heard. He gazed over at Jenny with panic clear in his gaze. "Jenny, do you mind if I go to have a look? It shouldn't take Erin this long."

Jenny swallowed nervously, rubbing at her belly in worry. Something wasn't right here. "No. Everyone else has already gone, and no one has come back. Please stay here, Matthew."

"Look, you're in the safest place," he urged. "Taraghlan is only back over there, so you're not alone. But Erin has gone in the wrong direction, I have to find her and...and maybe help her, I don't know. But we have to protect her above all else."

Shit. I know he's right. "Fine." Jenny gave a hard nod, biting back the fear that welled in her chest. "But please come back, even if you can't find her. We'll go find her together."

Matthew gave a reassuring smile in return, bobbing his head, and unsheathed his large claws. They screeched past bone as he grunted in pain, before he made his way silently through the leafy branches and trees after Erin. Jenny watched him, feeling silly for being so afraid. *He's right. I've nothing to fear here, it's just me and the girls.*

Flo rose up, gently placing Amber next to her, down onto the grass. She stretched luxuriously, raising her arms up towards the sky, yawning as she did so. She took a deep breath in, fluttering her eyes shut, as if savouring the sweet coolness of the night around her. Fixing her gaze on Jenny, she pushed her way through the shushing grass towards her. Jenny stared beyond her to Amber, expecting her to look sleepy or scared. Instead, the little girl sat with a strange smile on her face, almost beaming. Before Jenny had a chance to ask why, Flo was stood over her.

Jenny peered up with a ready smile, but it faded as Flo towered above her silently. Flo's features were cold and still, and her small fangs menacingly slid out from under her lip. Her lips curled into a cruel smile, as she stared down at the white face of Jenny.

Snapping into her fighting response, Jenny prepared to stand up, but she gave a grunt as the small teenager placed a hand on her shoulder and shoved her back to the hard ground. A frown creased between Jenny's eyes as she grimaced back up at Flo. "What the hell, Flo? Let me get up."

"Don't worry, Jenny," Flo whispered in reply, crouching down so that her melting silver eyes met Jenny's narrowed blue ones. "We'll look after you now."

Chapter Eight

Erin felt as though she had been walking for hours. *Surely the others couldn't have gone this far. And what the hell for? And why would they have left the girls alone?*

The questions tossed uneasily in Erin's head as she strode along, her feet making no noise on the green, mossy floor. Something wasn't right, but she couldn't put her finger on it. A bead of panic made its way up into her stomach, but she mentally pushed it away, moving on through the darkened woods.

She heard a crunch to the left of her, some distance away. She halted immediately, her pulse racing through her veins as she tightened her grip on Sioctine. Her eyes scanned the woods around her rapidly, trying to take in any movement at all. In the thick darkness she perceived a movement where she had heard the noise, a shadow that moved quickly and tried to hide behind a tree. Being as quiet as possible, Erin moved alongside the trunks, growing ever closer to the shadowy figure. She made out more of the figure; an arm, a face. As she slid along the rough bark of a tree, Sioctine gleamed menacingly in the dim light, Erin tightening her grip on the hilt. No further away than a couple of metres, Erin raised her sword, crouching to alter herself for the angle needed to cut towards the figure. As she drew in closer, and opened her mouth to speak—

"Get down!"

Erin went cold as the voice spoke to her.

"Get down!" the figure hissed again. It took a second for Erin to work out it was Taraghlan. She crouched down immediately, moving herself around to stare at his face, almost hidden in the dark shadow of the tall oak he leaned against.

"What the hell are you doing?" Erin hissed in reply, keeping Sioctine primed in front of herself.

Taraghlan sighed. "I heard you talking to the two girls with Jenny and Matthew. Something is off here, I can feel it."

Erin nodded. "Same here. It doesn't make any sense as to why they would wander off for no reason. And why would they leave Flo and Amber there?"

Taraghlan frowned. "You mean the others weren't there with them? Jenny and Matthew were alone?"

Erin shrugged. "It would seem that way. They weren't there when we arrived."

Taraghlan shook his head, biting his lip. "That definitely isn't right. I wanted to be sure she was safe, I shouldn't have come here. I thought it was just you who had wandered off."

A movement from the trees up ahead silenced both of them. Erin pointed over towards some rocks covered in moist green moss, and they both sneaked towards it, staying down. As they got closer, they heard muttering. Motioning for Taraghlan to stay where he was, Erin silently edged closer to the figure. The figure was laid on the floor, clutching at themselves. The muttering seemed disjointed and breathless. It was then she recognised the voice of the muttering figure. *Matthew. What the fuck is he doing here?!*

She beckoned over to Taraghlan, who quickly ran over. Erin sprinted over to Matthew's side, sliding Sioctine back into her sheath. Matthew was lying on his side, clutching at his stomach. Sticky, scarlet liquid pooled around him, soaking into the virgin moss beneath his torso. His eyes were closed, and his face was soaked in sweat as he muttered incomprehensibly to himself.

"Bloody hell! Matthew? Why are you here? I left you with Jenny and the girls."

Matthew weakly opened his eyes. As he saw Taraghlan and Erin's worried faces leaning over him, he grabbed Erin by her collar with his free hand, his eyes wide open and wild. "They...they...came from nowhere! It was...ambush...ambush!" He collapsed back to the floor, releasing her collar as he gasped in pain.

"What ambush? Who did this to you, Matthew?" Erin snapped, pulling his hand away from his torso to reveal a large tear in his stomach, skin and sinew torn away, blood pouring freely from the wound. Taraghlan pulled her hand away gently.

"Don't panic, he will heal from that. I've had worse," he reassured her. He peered back at Matthew, who was muttering away again. "Matthew? You must tell us what happened. Where are the others? Where is Jenny?"

Matthew frowned for a second, his eyes opening again. "Jenny?" he said, weakly. "She...she is with Flo and Amber, isn't she?"

Taraghlan's face drained of colour, and his eyes turned into ice. He grabbed Matthew's arm, shaking it hard. "Matthew, you left her alone with them?" He spoke through gritted teeth, clearly trying to swallow down the turmoil within himself. Erin pulled his arm away, pushing him back.

"Taraghlan! That isn't going to help. We'll go back for her now, don't panic." She turned back to Matthew, who tried to sit up, wincing in pain. She helped him up, leaning him against a tree, where he sighed in relief as he held his hand across his stomach wound. She crouched down in front of him, setting herself at eye level. Matthew opened his eyes fully, staring into Erin's weakly. "What happened to you? And where are the others? We need to know, quickly."

Matthew nodded, coming back into consciousness. He gritted his teeth and groaned as he pulled himself up further. "Well, you know Conner and Demitri ran off to take a look after the girls heard that scream, and you went off to find them, leaving me with the girls. You didn't return, so I got worried, and asked Jenny to stay with girls. I'm sorry, Taraghlan, I thought you were still at the camp."

Tara gave a grave nod, but his lips held in a firm line. "Understandable. I thought you were still with the girls."

Matthew licked his dry lips, swallowing as though to find saliva for his next words. "I...left the girls to run after them, Flo and Jenny said they would be fine. I got so far in. I saw Conner in the distance...he was running after something, or someone. I ran after them, and...something...someone...came out of nowhere, from the trees...they ripped me open, then...there were a few of them. But more than I could handle alone." He paused to take a breath, wincing as his wound shifted. "Bastards! I think they ripped out my intestines...this will take hours to heal up. I tried to fight, but there were so many. I heard Demitri and Conner shouting, then their voices grew faint. I tried to follow, but I wasn't able to keep up, so I tried to rest here. The pain was just too much." He paused and looked warily at Taraghlan. "I left Jenny with the girls though, she should still be there."

Taraghlan's face froze coldly. He stood up and

glared menacingly at the injured werewolf. "Matthew, if anything—*anything*—has happened to her, I shall take great pleasure in pulling your intestines back out of that wound in your stomach. And that is only to start with."

Anger poured from him in a torrent, Erin stood up to face him, placing her hand on her hilt as a warning. "Calm down, Taraghlan. Whatever has happened to the others, it wasn't Matthew's fault. Take your anger out on whoever is playing games with us right now. Come on, we had better take Matthew back to the girls and Jenny."

Taraghlan took a deep breath in and nodded, glancing away from Matthew back towards the camp. Taking Matthew between both of them, he leaned on Erin and Taraghlan's shoulders, hobbling along, stopping and groaning in pain every few moments. Erin noticed Taraghlan's delighted smirk every time Matthew winced, noting this with a shake of her head. *I understand how he feels about Jenny, but I still worry about that sadistic streak of his. I know he explained it to me, but it doesn't stop me fretting about it.*

As they neared the small clearing, twigs snapping and crunching beneath their feet, they smelt the fire and felt the cool breeze floating through the space before they noticed anything else.

Nobody was there.

The fire happily crackled away, eating hungrily at the remains of the wood it sat upon, sending strange flickering shadows dancing around the copse, and disappearing amongst the trees. The breeze floated through, flickering around the edges, tugging at the three figures stood at the edge of it. The moon had vanished, hiding behind a thick, protective grey cloud, barely moving in the windless sky.

"What the fuck? Where the hell are they? We left

Jenny with them." Erin stared cautiously around the trees, her stomach churning at being the mouse in this particular game of chase. Someone was toying with them, and she wasn't sure why. *If it was anyone from the castle, they would have captured us straight away, not played games like this.* She hurriedly hobbled Matthew over to the fire, with Taraghlan's help, and gently sat him down.

She shook her head. "What's going on? People disappearing left, right, and centre, people attacking in the middle of the woods...tell me this is some sort of nightmare." Her face turned ashen as she rasped, "They've got Jenny, as well. She was left here on her own with the girls."

Matthew shook his head heavily. "I don't know, but I can tell you this much. Someone has been following us, or watching us, or something. They're picking us off. I told you, an ambush. They're probably going to use the others as bait."

"Shit." Erin paced back and forth, running her hand through her hair. "She smacked her palm into her fist, her brows furrowing with worry. "What do we do first?" She stopped striding for a moment, gazing back towards Matthew and Taraghlan as if beseeching them for an answer. "Who do we look for first?"

Taraghlan raised his eyebrows as if it was a stupid question. "Jenny, obviously."

Erin snorted at him. "Why 'obviously'? Because you're worried about her over the others? How do you think I feel about Conner right now?" Her voice wobbled as she mentioned her mate's name. "Or Demitri?"

Taraghlan sighed, looking almost ashamed of himself for saying it. "I'm sorry, Erin. I didn't mean it that way. I know you are worried about him, but he can take care of himself. As can Demitri, and probably the girls too.

Jenny is a young human, she is more at risk of whatever is out there."

Erin bit her lip, and paced again, deep in thought. Her hand nervously fiddled with the hilt of her sword, her other hand running over and over her hair until she felt sure it would fall out of her head. Swallowing hard, she nodded slowly. "You're right, we need to go and find her first." Her voice cracked with pain. *I only just got him back. If something has happened to him, I'll never forgive myself, never.*

Matthew slowly edged himself up from the grass, wincing as he moved. He put a hand on Erin's shoulder. "Please try not to worry, Erin. Conner has been through much worse and survived. We will find him."

Erin turned around to face Matthew, her eyes bloodshot as she hemmed in her fear, and smiled wryly. "Thank you, Matthew, I know. I just...get afraid. I've only just found him again." Her eyes went blank for a second. She cleared her throat, willing herself back to her senses again. "Come on, then. We've got to find everyone, and I don't know where we're going to start."

Taraghlan's eyebrows furrowed as he bent down towards the dewy grass. Stiffening, he wiped across the fresh blades of greenery with his hand. His eyes melted into fury as he lifted his hand to his face. He turned towards Erin with a snarl. "Jenny's blood," he growled. "I'll kill them all. I'll fuc-"

"Enough," Erin snapped, blowing out a calming breath. "Can you follow the scent? Is there a trail?"

His breathing ragged, Taraghlan stared for a second at Erin before reluctantly calming himself, composing his cold face once more. "I'll see," he replied.

Matthew—already healing faster than Erin would have thought possible—and Erin moved closer to him, as he slowly and carefully made his way across the clearing, stopping every now and then to sniff the air, or touch the ground. He beckoned to both of them, urging them to follow him back into the darkness of the woods.

Chapter Nine

"What do you mean?" Jenny narrowed her gaze at Flo's silver eyes nervously, flinching at the coldness that had replaced her childlike innocence. Flo's lips stretched into a wide grin as she stared back at her silently.

Jenny glanced over towards Amber. The small girl simply giggled. Turning back to Flo, she made another attempt to stand, but was shoved back into the dirt, grazing her hands in the process. "Look, what the hell are you doing?"

Flo sat herself down next to Jenny, folding her skirt beneath her and sighing, almost happily. She clasped her hands in her lap, and turned to Jenny with her wide, cold smile. "You see, Jenny, we haven't been completely honest with you, or the others. My sister and I, we have been this way for the past...oh, two hundred years?" She grinned across at Amber, who was still giggling.

The seed of worry in Jenny's stomach blossomed into life and spread through her limbs, leaving every one of them tingling nervously. As Jenny turned her stare of astonishment over to Amber, Flo beckoned her over. Still baring the sweet, innocent face of a young child, Amber strode over. Gently, she put her small, chubby hand beneath Jenny's chin, pulling her face up towards hers so that she could look properly into her eyes.

"You see," Amber began, in a sweet, sing-song voice, "My 'bit' is to pretend that I'm a six-year old child. I cry a little, and I get upset, and I pout, and it makes everyone run towards me, to look after me." Her eyes narrowed, and the grip on Jenny's chin tightened. "Do you know — do you *understand* — how infuriating it is to be a grown women trapped in a child's body? And all because of those *fucking* werewolves!"

Flo cleared her throat, leaning into Jenny as if conferring a great secret upon her. "When Amber was very little, werewolves ransacked her village. Nearly everyone died. Those who didn't, such as Amber and myself, were turned. They brought us back from the brink of death. Unfortunately, when werewolves are created through turning, rather than being born, they do not age normally. We are stuck forever in these childish forms, while growing older within."

Amber released her hold on Jenny's chin as she stepped back, her eyes gleaming with a maturity Jenny hadn't noticed before, looking like no small child's eyes should ever look. "It can be quite useful though, as it was with you and your group. We lured you in, and you all fell for it, hook, line, and sinker. And now we're going to destroy all of you."

Jenny shook her head, thoughts whirling round so fast it seemed that she couldn't catch any of them, and hang on to any single one. "But why? What have we done to you?"

Flo glared sternly at her, the strange, cold smile still playing on her lips. "Well, not *you* personally, more your travelling companions. It's just unfortunate that you happened to be with them, we certainly didn't pinpoint you. We want to bring down Erin. And Conner, to a lesser extent."

"Bring them down? But they were helping you!"

"Too little, too late." Another voice rang out from

the depth of the woods, a voice that was harsh and unfeeling. As Jenny gulped back her trepidation, a man made his way into the moonlit clearing. He was staggeringly tall, dark, and handsome. But aside from his glowing silver eyes and cruel smirk, he was the double of Conner. Jenny let out a harsh gasp, shuffling backwards until her spine hit the tree behind.

As if he had heard the question passing through Jenny's mind, the man nodded at her. "Yes, I am familiar. I'm Conner's brother, Filtiarn. You know, the one he thought was *dead.*" The tall werewolf spat onto the ground beside his foot, as though the words had left an unpleasant taste in his mouth.

Amber and Flo stepped away as Jenny's eyes widened in shock. "But how can you be alive? He's thought he was Filtiarn—er, you, for hundreds of years! Taraghlan explained it all to me. You can't be Filtiarn."

The man seemed pleased as her stuttered words, and he flashed her a charming grin, his fangs slicing through. "Yes, I get that a lot. But you see, I had my eye on the biggest prize, all along. Play the long game, as it were. And now I will finally be rid of Conner, after so many centuries. And I will claim my prize." He turned his head for a moment, adding in a mutter, "Whatever my mother thinks."

Jenny rose up by holding onto the tree, her feet slipping on the damp grass, making her put her hand out quickly to prevent herself falling. She corrected herself and stood upright, fear and anger roiling in the pit of her soul at the strange tension that was building in the clearing, crackling around her like tiny fireworks. "Conner? Why would you want to kill him?"

The man sighed impatiently, running long fingers through his tousled jet-black hair. "Because he left me with nothing. First he took away the one thing I really wanted, then he pushed me out of my pack. You're a human, you have no idea what that's like. It's more than just being pushed away from your family. It pulls away something of yourself, saps your strength and courage. Now I'm going to take everything away from him."

Anger winning the battle over her panic, Jenny locked eyes with Flo and Amber, gritting her teeth at their smiles. "So they've been planted here to separate us all?" She jabbed a shaking finger towards them.

Filtiarn nodded gravely, the dark expression on his face lit up by the orange sparks that leapt away from the fire. "Of course. I was one of the very werewolves that turned them. All this time, Conner and Erin have been so wrapped up in their problems that they never noticed me roaming the world and collecting my own little pack together. When I found out you had all fled the castle, it seemed to be too good to be true. It was just so easy to take advantage of Conner's *good* nature."

Before Jenny had a chance to reply, Filtiarn beckoned to Flo and Amber, snapping his fingers at Jenny. "Enough. It's time to get rid of her. Make sure they don't find her, I want them to be flushed out like rats. You know who not to harm."

"Like shit, you will!" Jenny backed away, her footsteps slow and heavy at first. As Amber and Flo's grins became more grotesque, as their fangs slid out further and widened their smiles into snarls, Jenny's instincts finally kicked in. She twisted on her heels and dropped into a sprint, running through into the trees behind, every dark branch and twig seeming to try and slow her, slapping in her face. The darkness enveloped her as she ran further into the shadows, hearing Flo and Amber's light footsteps behind her, catching closer and closer with every breath she took.

Filtiarn grinned as he watched the three figures racing off, giving a pleased snarl. "One down, four to go."

Chapter Ten

After Conner and Demitri had ran for ten minutes, almost running round in circles, they paused and looked around in confusion. Conner turned to Demitri, who was breathing heavily, leaning over onto his knees. "Demitri, you did hear that as well, didn't you?"

Swallowing for air, Demitri stood upright and nodded quickly. "*Da*, I heard the shouts too."

Conner shook his head in dismay, placing his sword slowly back into its sheath. He couldn't work it out. They had heard the cries, and the yell, so close by…and yet a thorough search had revealed nothing. No footprints, no scent, no people. It was almost as though…

"Oh, shit." Conner grabbed Demitri's arm, pulling him downwards so that they were both crouched. Demitri pulled his arm loose indignantly, staring angrily at Conner's sudden loss of senses.

"What the hell are you doing?" he hissed. Conner put a finger to his lips, indicating silence. He tilted his head and scanned the area quickly, fearful someone might be listening to them.

"Demitri, I have a feeling this is a trap. We've left the others on their own, and no one was out here."

Demitri's eyes widened as the realisation of this sunk in slowly. "You're right—we need to get back!" Conner nodded and twisted around, as if to make his way back, when he froze. Demitri turned slowly as he caught the movement, dreading what might be there, and swore in shock.

Standing across from them was a young man with glowing silver eyes. He was the exact double of Conner. Everything was the same, from his coal-black hair to his sharply planed face. He towered over them, his wide eyes taking them in calmly as though the surprise was only on them, and he had expected them all along. Nobody spoke, the breeze seeming to hold still with everyone's breath, until Conner spoke up in faltering voice. "Fil...Filtiarn?"

"Filtiarn? I thought he was dead?" Demitri hissed.

"So did I," Conner replied, his tone low as he gave a hard swallow.

Filtiarn shook his head determinedly, his eyes glowing. "You're going to find out a lot of things were not as you thought. You have to come with me, it's not safe here."

Conner paused. "No, I...I don't know what's going on here, but we need to go back for the girls. We must-" He roved his eyes once again over his brother. *What the hell is going on? I'd swear my mind was playing tricks on me again if Demitri couldn't see him.*

"Look, you haven't got time. We'll go back for them, but right now you must come with me, or you won't be here to come back *for* them."

Demitri glanced at Conner, who gazed back at him doubtfully, his insides twisting in worry. "What do you think?"

Conner shook his head, sweat forming on his palms as he fought between logic and his need to keep Erin safe. "I don't know, I can't think."

"*Now!* If we stay here much longer, they'll find you, come on!" Filtiarn urged once more, beckoning them to follow him.

"From who?"

"Look, I'll explain later. You—you're been chased by werewolves sent by our mother. You have been since you left the castle, I've been watching you. You have to come with me now, there are far too many of them."

Demitri's eyes turned steely. "Your mother?"

Conner looked back at Filtiarn, the twin brother he had thought dead for so long. *Can I trust him?* He cast his gaze from his brother's dark hair, down to the firm line of his mouth and silvery eyes. "This is so strange. I thought...I thought we'd all lost you. But you're right, this can come later. Let's go."

Demitri grabbed his arm with a desperate grip. "Conner, are you sure?"

Conner let out a low breath, still holding his twin's intense stare. "No. But I think we have to."

Conner stepped into the small, ruined house. It had once been part of the village at the edge of the woods, now bombed to shreds by the recent battles. The back end of the house still contained two small rooms with walls and a roof. One was a kitchen, and he made his way through after Filtiarn and Demitri, sinking down onto a nearby barstool that lived on at a haphazard angle.

It was a country-style kitchen, with maple front units and a large wooden kitchen table in the centre. Four turned kitchen chairs were placed around the table, one of them missing half of its back. The walls were painted a pale yellow, now covered in a spray of black soot and ash. The back door had a large plywood board nailed hurriedly across the space where a window used to sit, now smashed through. There was no humming from the fridge, as the electricity was still off, adding to the eerie silence of the room. Several candles were lined up along one of the kitchen worktops, some nearly burnt down to the wick, others dribbling their waxy contents over the edges. The kitchen tap dripped a steady, almost merry tune against the tarnished metal sink. The washbowl sat within the sink, half twisted and melted, still containing a few smashed pieces of crockery.

Filtiarn rummaged around one of the cupboards, muttering to himself and throwing various packages and boxes either out onto the floor, or onto the worktop above him like an animal scavenging for scraps. He finally stood up, selecting a few of the packets and scrutinising the list at the side of each with intensity. He glanced over towards Demitri and Conner as if remembering he had someone with him for the first time. "Biscuits? There isn't much else here, I've eaten most of what was still okay to eat."

Right on cue, Demitri and Conner's stomachs rumbled loudly, answering for them. Conner grinned. "That would be great. We haven't eaten anything for a while."

Filtiarn nodded again, a strange, quick nod that was almost that of a nervous animal. He pulled some newspapers from the top, yellowing and wrinkled, showing how long they had been there for. Beneath were a mismatch collection of plates and cups. He grabbed one of the plates, throwing a quantity of the biscuits onto it, quickly placing it onto the table. He then grabbed three cups of varying sizes and designs, one of them cracked and split, pacing over to the dripping tap and spraying water into each one. He came back over to the table, sitting himself down and putting a cup in front of Demitri and Conner, leaving the cracked one for himself. He shrugged apologetically, adding, "Sorry, it's the only thing there is to drink."

"*Eto preknashno.* This is perfect, thank you." Demitri raised his cup to Filtiarn, gratefully taking a large swallow of the mineral tasting water.

Conner bent his head in reply, and took a deep drink of the water. *That has never tasted better in my life. I didn't realise how thirsty I was.* His head swam with a headache that forced its way through, as though the water had brought some life back to his tired body. He set his cup down onto the worn table, gently tracing the lines that had been made long ago by a chopping knife. He gazed back up at Filtiarn with a held breath, still disbelieving that the eyes he stared at were his brother's. "Filtiarn, are you going to tell me what is going on? I thought you were dead. Fucking *dead.* So did everyone else, as far as I know. Where have you been all this time? I went to see your *grave,* for fuck's sake! We were told that you had been ripped apart by humans. It's the reason that I invented you again, inside my head, the reason Erin came after me...the reason for this whole bloody mess! Why are you here? And why didn't you come to find us? Where have you been?"

Filtiarn slowly lowered the biscuit he had raised to his mouth, and cleared his throat. "Er...locked up?"

"Locked up?"

"Yes...after I left the village, our mother...she came after me. She told me that she had somewhere safe for me to go, and that she would talk Erin around to letting me back. She took me to this small house. It was gatehouse of some kind, to a manor —her house. She shut me in the rooms there, and, well...never came back. I was locked in for centuries. It was only recently I escaped, and I've been hiding out here since the war began."

"Wait." Conner held his hand up to stop him, closing his eyes for a second as he leaned onto the table with his elbow. "That doesn't make any sense. How did you survive locked in for several centuries?"

"Lot of rats in there," Filtiarn replied, grimly. He shrugged again. "I think she meant for me to die there. Now I think about it."

Demitri leaned in, holding the cup of water tightly in his hand, furrowing his brow in thought. "You survived...on rats?"

Filtiarn nodded, shoving another biscuit into his mouth. He swallowed it quickly, brushing the crumbs away from the table in front of him. "You get used to it. Sometimes other animals would crawl in, bigger things. I didn't like it, but what else could I do? I couldn't get out. She used magic on the locks."

He cleared his throat and swallowed another mouthful of water, his eyes remaining fixed on his two guests. "Anyway, when the war started, some of the bombs landed on the house. There were stones everywhere, but I took refuge in the tunnels beneath — they're all closed off, but I could use some of them. They led up to the old manor house, it was for the servants, or emergencies, or something. Who knows? These old places were always built with escape tunnels. Once it quieted down, I came out, and found myself in the manor house. It was...amazing. I hadn't seen proper sunlight for over a thousand years. Not out in the open, anyway. It was gleaming off everything...trees, grass — the sky itself was almost too bright to look at. I heard voices, arguing, so I decided I would take a look. It was our mother, arguing with someone about capturing you and Erin." He pointed at Conner as he said this, sternly looking at him. "Wait, what did you mean by you 'invented' me in your head?"

Conner cast a strained look over at Demitri, who shrugged in reply. "It's...a long story. I missed you so much, and felt so guilty about your death, that I...I began to imitate you a little. Well, it was a sort of schizophrenia, I guess. Rosa decided to take advantage of this. She's still angry at Erin and myself, so she decided she was going to make an attempt at destroying us. She put an enchantment on me so that I developed a split personality, one being myself, the other being you. Well, *you* amplified by about a hundred."

"An enchantment? Wait, you're not still like that?" Filtiarn crunched on a biscuit, staring anxiously at Conner.

Conner shook his head determinedly, replying, "No, I got it removed. By her, no less. She took the enchantment off, but..." he bit his lip, sucking back the venom as he spoke of her. "She's still trying to kill us off, or something. Our father said as much—yes, I met him too. But don't worry about a family reunion, he's dead now. We were going to hunt her down too."

Another mouthful of biscuit falling from the corner of his mouth, Filtiarn shook his head. "Yup, I heard her saying something about that when she was speaking to these other werewolves in the forest. Something about getting her husband to join her."

Demitri gave a short, cold laugh. "Well, good luck with that. He is most definitely dead. We all saw it."

Filtiarn stared at him, holding his breath. "Good riddance. There's something else, though. You were tricked by the two she was arguing with. They looked like little girls."

Conner's blood ran cold as he swallowed back fear, a shiver running along his spine. "Wait, those two were harmless. They were barely old enough to walk around on their own."

Filtiarn shook his head again, sighing. "No, those

two are a lot older than they look. I could smell them from where you were. They might look young, but they're centuries old. I'm surprised you didn't scent it, but I guess you weren't looking for it. I've been watching you tonight. I wanted to come over, but...I wasn't sure how. They're working for *her.*"

"Why would they be working for her?" Conner tapped his fingers on the wooden table top, his leg twitching in impatience. He knew Filtiarn meant his mother, but it didn't make as much sense as it seemed on the surface. *So she separates us by using her little werewolves. So what? There's only two of them, the others will have them down before they get to grip their fangs in. And then what? She's left on her own, with no one to help her.*

Filtiarn stared blankly at Conner, his expression twisting with confusion. He tilted his head to one side, narrowing his gaze. "You really don't know, do you?" he asked in a hushed voice. "She isn't like our father, Conner. She is something else."

Conner sighed in exasperation. This was going much slower than he would have hoped. Filtiarn sat in front of him still didn't seem real. *But with our fucked-up family...anything's possible.* "Care to share with me what that is?"

Filtiarn swallowed with obvious unease. "She is...not entirely werewolf. She's got powers, Conner. Powers that most witches alive today can only dream of. Apparently, she was a witch long before she was a werewolf."

"How?" Conner clasped and unclasped his hands to get feeling back into them as the situation weighed into him, sending crackles of tension running along his nerves. Unable to sit still any longer, he jumped up from his seat, pacing around the small kitchen. "What does it matter?"

Finishing the last of his sugary meal, Filtiarn scraped back his chair to face Conner, shaking his head. "Don't you understand? It's how she's done everything to us. The magic she uses isn't borrowed from some other witch, she uses other witches when she doesn't want to get her hands dirty. And they're not just parlour tricks, either. Remember how Erin left the pack to come and find you?"

"Well, I know of it."

"That was our mother's doing. She forced Erin to go find you, then took over the pack. She created a new race of werewolves by using magic—not pure werewolves, like you and I, but vicious creatures who only wanted blood. Her ambition burns as bright as ever. Whatever she's up to, Conner...she wants the pack for herself again."

Demitri raised his eyebrows in amazement, slowly taking another sip from the cup in front of him. He stared at Conner, unblinking. "You have a weird family, Conner."

"Tell me about it." Conner's tone was weak. There was too much information at once, too much to digest. "Shit. We can't let her do this. We have to kill her, *now*. We must go back for Erin and the others, and I won't argue about it." This last sentence was said to Filtiarn, holding up a hand in warning. Demitri and Filtiarn watched him avidly as he strode back and forth, rubbing his mouth every now and then, his brows furrowed in deliberation. He paused for a second, staring out of the soot-covered kitchen window across the vast countryside beyond. *But where would she be?*

"Where are these...feral werewolves, at the moment?"

Clearing his throat, Filtiarn stood up, and pointed across the kitchen, to an imaginary point. "They're in the woods. The manor I told you about? That's where they're staying, I think. As far as I know, she won't travel too far from them. It's her army, after all."

Conner looked over at Demitri, his eyes lit up with anticipation. "Then we must go there first. Either Erin will be there with them, or she'll still be hidden from them, and we can root out the problem at the source. They want a war, they'll get one...Rosa will be gone before daybreak."

Filtiarn slid off his seat as Demitri and his brother made their way from the ruined kitchen, holding back the bubble of excitement that threatened to burst from his chest. They both wore grim expressions, and all he wanted to do was throw back his head and laugh. Masking the wicked thrill running through his body, keeping his face straight, Filtiarn moved ahead of them and led the way. *They're going to do it for me. Now I don't even have to get my hands dirty.*

As he came out into the burst of warm afternoon sun, he cocked his head over his shoulder and gave Conner what he hoped was a reassuring smile. Conner grinned back, but it seemed forced. *Hmm...put it down to the situation. After all, it's not often your dead brother turns up again, is it?* His eyes hardened to steel as he leapt over a low red brick wall, heading back to the woods, in the direction of the manor house on the hill. He would get his prize yet. And his mother still had no idea.

Chapter Eleven

Erin had picked up the scent herself, a strange, metallic smell that permeated every tree and plant around them. It was too thick, too fresh, as if there should never be that much of the scent at once. Matthew followed behind her, already well on the way to healing, the gaping tear in his stomach slowly weaving itself back together again.

Ahead of her, Taraghlan hurriedly made his way through the trees, pausing every now and then to scan the area before continuing, seeming possessed by his search. Erin was about to ask him how much further he imagined Jenny could be, when he held up a hand. He sniffed the air tensely, like a dog searching for the scent of danger. As if he had suddenly been greeted by a wavering, smoky finger of smell, leading him the right way, he raced off to the left, running only a few metres.

Casting a quick, worried glance at one another, Erin and Matthew chased after him, skirting around the trees until they came upon a horrific sight. Erin stopped in horror, her hand flying to her mouth. Taraghlan knelt in the grass, his shoulders shaking with uncustomary sobs, his hand gently stroking something. As Erin gazed down, she saw that he was stroking the hair of Jenny, prone in the grass, her face twisted into an exclamation of terrible pain. All around her, blood and flesh were strewn about the mossy undergrowth, the nearby trees covered in dripping scarlet liquid, the vague imprint of hands occasionally appearing. Jenny's body was covered in scratches and tears, limbs ripped open, and precious bodily fluids poured from every open seam.

"Oh, Taraghlan," Erin whispered, falling to her knees behind him. Matthew leaned against a tree, shaking his head repeatedly in shock.

"My little Jenny," Taraghlan rasped. "I should never have tried to bring you back this time. Not this time. And now you're gone again." A single tear, a phenomenon that had never been seen on his cheek for centuries, trickled down and splashed onto her cold white cheek.

As it did so, she stirred, her eyelids fluttering in agony.

Erin gripped Taraghlan's arm with a clawed hand, breathing heavily with tense excitement. "Taraghlan, she's still alive!"

Taraghlan nodded, cradling Jenny's head in his arm. "Thank the gods!" He traced his fingers over her face, and Jenny groaned, but it sounded distant and strained. His face fell again, and he swallowed hard. "But barely. Oh, little Jenny, I've got you back." As Erin watched, he brought his hand to his mouth, preparing to slice it open with his teeth.

"What the hell are you doing?" Erin hissed in shock, making him pause for a second to look blankly at her.

"I'm saving her. Don't give me that look, Erin. Her heartbeat is weak, I can feel it. I must make her like me. I must save her. I can't lose her again."

Erin's face tautened, glancing down at Jenny's barely breathing form as she bit back her worry. "What do you mean, losing her *again*? You can't do it, what if she...what if this isn't what she wants?"

Taraghlan gripped Jenny closer, running his spare hand through the chestnut hair that spilled across his lap to meet the green beneath them. His eyes grew silver and cold as he hissed in return, "You think you're the only one who lost your soulmate? What if for the past thousand years, your soulmate had been born human. And you knew her, recognised her even before you knew her name. And to know you could never have her? To watch her grow old with a man who didn't deserve her? To watch her die again and again in a cruel cycle? Jenny has always been watched over by me, every time she was reincarnated. But this is the first time I ever got a true taste, a true glimpse into what might be. I won't give that up, not this time. And she's going to die anyway, at least I'll be giving her a chance—and she agreed to be with me. For the first time in centuries, Erin, I felt alive with her by my side. I felt..." His voice cracked, and he added, "I felt like I could be someone she would be proud of, instead of the monstrous creature I've been for so long. I don't care how we have to work it out, she is my little Jenny. If she decides it's not what she wants, and she doesn't want to be with the pack..."He paused again, and took a deep, shaky breath, "I'll disappear with her. We'll both disappear, and I'll watch her forever. As long as she is with me. Wouldn't you do the same for Conner?"

An eternity seemed to pass by as Erin looked deep into Taraghlan's eyes. He was sincere, she could see that, and she could see the pain and torment of watching the women he loved cruelly taken from him again and again by fate for hundreds of years. *But if she doesn't want it...no, Jenny isn't like that. She would want to live. And he's right. If it was me in his place...I'd do it for Conner. A hundred times over, no matter the cost.* She closed her eyes for a second, trying to steady the spinning thoughts within her mind, before nodding slowly. "Alright, do it," she said, moving back to sit on the mossy floor.

Taraghlan muttered his thanks, a smile almost meeting his lips as he bent over Jenny. Erin glanced over at Matthew, her heart thumping in her mouth. He nodded back at her, his silent agreement that she had made the right decision. All werewolves, whether they had found their mates or not, knew the pain of losing one. It wasn't like losing a limb. It was worse than that. It was like losing oxygen, or water. Werewolves often perished by their own hand after losing a mate.

The breeze gently flapped the loose leaves on the branches above them, a strange, whistling tune erupting from some of the larger leaves, as if singing. Small noises could be heard from the moss-covered undergrowth, a city of small insects busily continuing with everyday life, whatever the upstairs world was doing. A bird sang out somewhere distant amongst the trees, abruptly stopping, as if he too felt the hopeful air that surrounded the young woman.

A low groan came from Jenny's mouth, and her lips moved noiselessly. Taraghlan hugged her closer to him, shushing her moving lips with his finger. "Don't talk, darling. Rest for now," he muttered, his voice wavering.

Jenny took a deep breath, as if it were the first breath she had ever taken, stirring as her arm reached up to stroke Taraghlan's cheek. "They...they ran...I was too...too slow..." her arm fell again to rest by her side. She took another deep, shaking breath, swallowing at the same time.

"Ssh." Taraghlan stroked her hair gently, rocking her in his arms as he cradled her close to his chest. His face was pinched with emotion, but his lips were curved into a warm smile as he looked down at his mate.

Erin stood up, brushing the loose leaves from the seat of her jeans, her shoulders cracking from stiffness as she rose up. Matthew looked over to her, breathing heavily. "What now? We can't stay here."

Erin nodded. "But we can't just go either. What if the others come back and need to find us? We should leave something—"

Taraghlan scoffed. "What, like Hansel and Gretel? Leave a trail of breadcrumbs here, and there will be more than werewolves coming after you."

Erin sighed, pinching her forehead between finger and thumb as she forced her brain to come up with a plan. She was tired and weary from the last few days, and a lack of water and food was taking a toll on her and the others, no matter how immortal they were. Gritting her teeth together, she willed an idea to spring forth. *There must be something…some way to let them know we're here, some way to—*

Erin was jarred from her thoughts by Jenny growing more animated, reaching up for Taraghlan once more. "We must…go…we must—"

"No, ssh." Taraghlan tried to sooth her again, his attempt being met by Jenny weakly pushing his arm away, shaking her head in frustration.

"No! Listen…listen…the two girls…they are not…they're with him…they attacked me…Flo and Amber attacked me…they were with a man…he told them…told them…" Jenny stopped talking, breathing heavily with the exertion, swallowing in great lumps of air.

Taraghlan turned and cast a cold, steely look at Erin. "Those girls were trouble. And we let them into our group. Allowed them to tear into *Jenny!*" His voice ended on a roar, but he was stopped by Jenny moaning and reaching for him once more, making him return to soothing and petting her frantically.

Erin cleared her throat. "Well, we can't stay here. We must find somewhere to stay for the rest of the night, somewhere that Matthew and Jenny can recuperate. That is the main priority. Then we have to think of the others…we have to find them, but we're no good to them at the moment."

Taraghlan nodded, placing his hand beneath Jenny's knees, gently lifting her and pulling her in closer to his chest. He whispered something into her hair, closing his eyes for a second, opening them again to gaze at his two other companions as he turned around.

Matthew broke in, wincing as he twisted his body. "But where are we going to go? We can't go back to the camp, and they probably have most of these woods covered."

Erin nodded. "I know that. But I saw a small village on the way in, there were some ruined houses. I think we should make our way towards those, they should be a little bit safer than here. Then we'll come back in the morning." She paused for a moment, waiting to see if there were any arguments to her suggestion, before continuing, "Alright, let's go then. This way."

The sun was awakening, its sleepy rays piercing through the quiet trappings of night. Birds, somewhere off in the canopy of trees, began to sing merrily, breaking through the fear and cold of the previous night. In Erin's head, it all seemed like a nightmare. It didn't seem real. Even after all the events leading up to this point, the night in the woods seemed the most surreal. *You go for one walk in the woods, and everyone ends up disappearing, just because*

we allowed two traitors into the group. But why? Who were they? Why do all this? The answer came to her so fast that she answered her own question as soon as she asked it. *Rosa.*

She kicked herself inwardly for allowing them to come along, thinking that they were alone and abandoned because of her own doing. *All because of my guilt. I won't make that mistake again. No one outside our group is to be trusted.* She had the strange feeling that she had told herself that piece of advice a long time ago.

They finally came out of the woods, the tall trees getting shorter and eventually giving way to a gravel path, which in turn became a short country road. The four of them marched along it, Jenny resting in Taraghlan's arms, their feet crunching until they came to a small village.

It was a terrible sight in the morning sun. Houses were half-demolished, some completely collapsed to the ground. Half-snapped trees adorned what remained of gardens, and a car merrily burned away outside a large cottage, its front wheels completely gone. An acrid smell filled the air, drifted along by the breeze that picked up around them, lifting their hair playfully. As they stared, there was a snapping, groaning sound as a nearby garage roof collapsed inwards and crashed to the ground, lifting a great cloud of smoke from the dusty floor.

Holding their breath against the burnt scent that filled their lungs, the group made their way further into the village. Erin pointed at one house, a small end-of-terrace building that looked to be in one piece, with the exception of its front windows, which were clean smashed through and half-boarded up with loose plywood and nails. They made their way across the garden that was left, stepping over smoking pieces of rubble and flowers torn to shreds, blood scattered in great ribbons across the dying brown grass. Gently trying the door handle, Erin pushed the front door open, expecting to feel some resistance, but instead the door easily swung open with an almost silent squeak of its hinges.

The hallway was dark, only fragments of light making their way through the nailed-up boards to greet the dusty carpets within. Coughing at the rising particles of dust, Erin beckoned the others through, closing the door behind them as they came in, after taking a quick scan outside of the house. Trudging through the living room floor, scattered with ripped magazines and torn carpet showing a vague blue rose pattern, they made their way over to the sofas, more dust erupting in the beams of light and floating across the room.

Taraghlan gently placed Jenny down on one of the sofas, Matthew seating himself on the other one, sighing and closing his eyes with relief as he did so. Erin looked over at Jenny as Taraghlan rose up. "How long will it take?"

Taraghlan shrugged, his gaze still fixated on Jenny's sleeping form. "I don't know. It could take hours, or days. She'll pass in and out of consciousness until then."

Erin nodded and plumped herself down on the sofa next to Matthew. Taraghlan eased himself next to Jenny, cradling her once more. "Okay, there's no way Jenny can come with us right now, and Matthew is still in bad shape, so he'll have to stay and watch her."

"Hell, no!" Taraghlan jumped up from the sofa, making Jenny stir. "He already fucked up once, remember? He was left with her and he went bounding off after a yell in the trees—what if this time a roof tile falls off the house? Is he going to go running after that?"

Erin glanced over at Matthew, who cast his eyes

to the ground in an ashamed manner. "I'm sorry, I didn't know…I'm sorry."

"He's sorry," Taraghlan scorned. He gazed over at Erin with burning eyes, his mouth drawn tight. "I am *not* leaving her with him."

Erin sighed heavily with exasperation, glaring at Taraghlan. "Fine. Then there is only one other option. I'll go, and you three stay here—and try not to kill each other?"

Matthew tried to protest, but Erin shook her head sternly, pointing a finger at him. "No arguments, Matthew. It's the only thing we can do right now. I'm not happy leaving anybody here, but you and Jenny can't come with us, and it would be best if someone else was here to look after both of you." She paused and looked fiercely at Taraghlan. "And I mean *you*. If I get back and things here are anything but peachy and rosy, I'll separate your head from your shoulders myself. Besides, if I go myself, there is less chance of them being able to track us. I can handle myself. I am an Alpha, in case anyone has forgotten." She made her way over to the door, and took a glance over her shoulder. "Is that clear?"

Both Matthew and Taraghlan nodded curtly, Matthew looking less happy than Taraghlan.

Nodding in return, Erin blew out a calming breath. She had a horrible feeling in the pit of her stomach about this, but she had no choice. Straightening herself up, she gripped Sioctine firmly with her hand, the good, heavy feeling of cool metal leaning against her leg. Opening the door with nothing more than a creak, she strode outside into the cool air.

Chapter Twelve

"It's over there," Filtiarn hissed, pointing through the bushes. A once grand manor house stood before them, great grey blocks of stones making up the huge frontage. Ebony wood windows stared down, empty eyes of the house, while the magnificent dark doors at the front of the manor were thrown open, the ornate carvings upon them glinting in the early sunlight. A whole section of the house was crumbled away on one side though, a ruinous mass of bricks and stone. Two figures stood outside the manor doors, dressed up in gleaming black uniforms and hoods.

Conner nodded towards them with a snort. "What's with the fancy get up?"

Filtiarn glanced over, chuckling grimly. "Those are her guards. I imagine she wanted them to look a certain way. She has her little ways."

Demitri sniffed derisively. "So how do we get into this place?"

Filtiarn grinned mischievously and pointed downwards. "Through the sewers."

"Through the sewers?" Conner interjected. "Where did you get that idea from, a bad action film? There must be another way in."

Filtiarn stared at him coldly. "Oh, there is. You can go running over to those guards there, and see how many you can rip apart before they get enough of them to stop you and do something far more horrific."

Conner groaned through gritted teeth. "Fine. Where is the entrance to these sewers?"

Pointing, Filtiarn turned his gaze towards the side of the house, where the group could see a large grate, covered with overgrown weeds and grass. "Through there. That's the entrance that leads down into the main sewers. From there, we can head to the centre of the house from the kitchen sewers."

Nodding to the others, Filtiarn sneaked his way alongside the edge of the woods, keeping himself hidden in the long grass. It swayed gently as he passed, but made no sound. Conner followed him, Demitri not far behind. The two guards at the entrance of the manor made no movement, still staring ahead into the distance.

As they came closer in line with the sewer grate, Filtiarn bent down to inspect the iron bars. After searching them for a moment or two, he leaned back, whispering, "It has large screws fixing it to the wall, it'll take me a minute or so to get them off."

"Well, go on then," Conner hissed back urgently. Filtiarn nodded hurriedly and turned back, bending down to twist off the first of the screws. As he turned his attention to the next one, Demitri placed his hand on Conner's arm.

"Conner, can you hear that? Someone is coming near."

Conner glanced at him in shock before twisting his head and listening intently. Demitri was right. Someone was making their way slowly from round the back of the house, their footsteps steadily making their way through the long grass.

Conner tapped Filtiarn fervently on the back. "Hurry up!" he rasped. "What's taking so long?"

Filtiarn hissed back at him, "I'm going as quickly

as I can, one of the screws is stuck. I'm trying to loosen it."

Conner peered back at Demitri, whose face was drawn and pale. Demitri swallowed loudly, and glanced over at the rapidly growing louder approach of the boots on the overgrown gardens. He gripped Conner's shoulder tightly. "I'll go and take care of them."

Conner pulled him back, keeping his other hand steady on his sword hilt. "No, you stay here. There could be more than one of them round there. If they come around here, we'll deal with it then." Conner's heart thumped in his mouth as he listened to the steady thudding of the footsteps getting closer, sweat forming under his tight grip of his sword until—

"I've got it! Let's get in," Filtiarn whispered triumphantly, lifting the grate upwards and wincing as it creaked.

As the grate screeched, the footsteps stopped in response. The guard had heard them. "Shit!" Conner grabbed Demitri and yanked him over to the grate. Filtiarn had already jumped in. A light splashing of water could be heard from lower down. Demitri slid in next, after a worried glance at Conner. Conner urged him in, his eyes widening in anticipation. A second later, Conner slid in after him, pulling the grate shut after himself, just as he caught a glimpse of someone's foot appearing around the corner of the house.

He slid down into a seating position, closing his eyes in the darkness and breathing heavily, his pulse thumping in his ears. As he opened his eyes, allowing them to adjust to the black interior of the sewer, he leaned over and grabbed Filtiarn by his shirt, who was leaning back and watching him.

"If you...ever..." he swallowed a breath. "...ever, do that again, I'll kill you myself. We are not here for a game. If they catch us, we die, and so does everyone else."

Filtiarn snarled, pulling Conner's hand off. "Hey, I know that. Don't grab me again. I understand what's at stake here, more than you think I do."

"Which way do we go now?" Demitri hissed, breaking up the conversation and pointing forwards into the depths of the damp, slimy tunnel before them.

Filtiarn thought for a second and nodded towards the tunnel ahead of them. "We follow this tunnel until we come to another one on our left. That will lead us into the drains below the kitchens, and we'll sneak in that way."

Conner nodded, and gestured for him to lead the way. Filtiarn edged forwards, slowly disappearing in the dim lighting of the tunnel. Conner and Demitri heard him fumbling about on the wall next to them. An orange electric light suddenly buzzed into life in front of them, making them blink rapidly as it burned into their retinas. As their sight cleared, they could see that Filtiarn was grinning and holding up a small electric lamp. "They always leave some of these down here," he whispered. "This will make it much easier."

He turned on his heel and continued to wade through the sewers, the soft splashing resounding from the concrete walls. The buzzing of insects echoed from some of the dimmer parts of the sewers, followed by a revolting smell that made their eyes sting.

Without saying anything, Filtiarn noiselessly pointed to his left, placing a finger to his lips in a shushing motion. He passed the lamp to Demitri, who held it up so that the group could see what they had stopped at. It was another entrance grate, except it was smaller than the first one, and lower down. Voices could be heard from above, travelling down with an icy breeze that swirled and eddied in the dank dampness of the sewers.

Filtiarn carefully loosened the screws of the grate, placing each one into his pocket so as not to make any extra noise. Any unnecessary noise at that point would travel up through the grate to the house above. Conner leaned over to hold the grate steady as Filtiarn loosened the final screw, placing it into his pocket. He quickly grabbed the other side of the grate, lifting it with Conner, and both of them placed it down on the other side of the tunnel.

Filtiarn took the lamp from Demitri again, feeling around on the ceiling with his spare hand, until he gave a triumphant sound. Lifting the lamp upwards, he hung it from the nail sticking out from the ceiling, leaving it swinging as it cast shadows across the tunnel. Silently nodding at Conner and Demitri, who gestured back in return, he crouched down and crawled into the small tunnel leading up to the kitchens.

Demitri followed him, taking a deep breath before going in, and Conner brought up the rear. He gave the tunnel around him a last look, checking to see that no one was following them, before bending down to creep into the small tunnel.

He couldn't see much in front, but he could make out the dark figure of Demitri in front of him, and occasionally Filtiarn's leg. He tried to crawl slowly, keeping as soundless as possible. His hand nearly slipped for a second as he reached out and met something cold and slimy, a burst of rancid smell breaking out and greeting him. He stilled, slowly pulling his hand back and wiping whatever it was on his trousers, before continuing as he held his breath as well as he could. The voices grew louder as they grew closer, a few words escaping into the recesses of the sewer.

"...no, down in the rooms..."

"...don't know why she's here. Perhaps she's..."

"...need to keep it secret..."

"...he said to find her. Destroy her..."

Conner wondered who they were talking about. Erin? An icy rush of fear zipped through his veins again, and he mentally shook the thought away. *I mustn't think about that. Not right now, or I'll go mad. Concentrate on this.*

Filtiarn motioned for the other two to stop, and looking ahead, Conner could see that his brother had reached the grate in the floor of the manor kitchen. Filtiarn pressed his face as close as he dared to try and see as far into the room as he could. Conner peered over his shoulder, taking in as much as he could see. His eyes first met a tiled terracotta floor, surrounded by wooden kitchen cabinets. No more than a few metres away, two pairs of thick army boots stood. Whoever the werewolves were, they appeared to be complaining about someone.

The first voice to speak was female, but sounded as though she was pushing gravel through her tired vocal chords. "I don't understand why we have to speak to her. Surely she isn't needed?"

A throat was cleared, and a deep, male voice responded, "Perhaps. But it's not up to us to decide what we need to do. The Alpha understands what he is doing. After all, he has got us this far, hasn't he?"

"Yes, that's true." The female voice giggled. "Yes, in fact, we're sat here in this cosy house while the other werewolves fall about and tear each other apart, leaving us to take over and restore order for them."

The male voice joined in the laughter, agreeing, "Yes, that's true! But not like last time." The laughter died away as he rasped, "This time will be different."

In the sewer below, both Conner and Demitri gritted their teeth, but remained silent. Filtiarn eyed them wearily. There was a sharp movement from above as somebody scraped a chair out, moving their feet across the tiles. The male appeared to have stood up, and was stretching luxuriously.

"I'm off to complete a round of the manor. Beckfield radioed a while ago to say he thought he saw someone going into the sewers...I told him to cool down on going outside in the sun for a while. The air is obviously getting to him."

"Hah! Obviously. I'll see you later. I'll be checking up on the prisoner soon."

"Great." A hand appeared over the far end of the kitchen, stooping to pick up a black helmet from the kitchen work surface. Conner listened until he heard the steady footsteps of the heavy boots disappearing, and the kitchen door was slammed shut. He waited for a few moments, listening to the other figure as he placed a hand on Filtiarn's shoulder to hold him back.

The female figure hummed to herself for a few minutes before pulling her chair back, and following her companion out of the kitchen door, clicking it firmly shut behind herself. Filtiarn craned his head, as if being completely sure that he could hear no more sounds. Bracing himself, he pushed at the kitchen grate carefully until it gave way, and came out with a dull clang. Demitri and Conner winced, but no one came, and no sound of boots could be heard.

Lifting himself out of the cramped tunnel, Filtiarn sat on the tiled floor and leaned back to offer a hand to Demitri. He helped to pull him clean out, and both of them leaned back to helped Conner out. As he came out of the tunnel, he stretched his six-foot plus frame, grimacing at the clicks his spine made.

The kitchen appeared to be completely normal,

with the exception of any form of utensils or appliances. It was dirty and dusty, but nothing to show anyone lived here. Filtiarn ran over and threw the door open, checking the tiny view he had of the hallway outside. Conner and Demitri waited until he beckoned them over before edging across to him. The hallway beyond was beautifully decorated, a rich green carpet running along the length of the long passageway, gilded wallpaper hanging from the high walls, crystal chandeliers hanging from the high carved ceilings.

Pointing at a door further down the corridor, Filtiarn whispered, "That's where we need to be. That room there is where their leader sits."

Chapter Thirteen

"ome on," Filtiarn whispered, beckoning for Demitri and Conner to follow him. He quietly crept out into the passageway, Demitri and Conner glancing at one another in trepidation before following. Filtiarn paced along the corridor until he came to an open door. He turned back and hissed, "I can hear someone coming. Quick, get in here!" He burst the door open, holding for his two followers to get in as well. Conner followed Demitri in, frowning. *I can't hear anyone.*

Once they were in, Filtiarn shut the door behind them. Before Conner got a chance to speak to him about it, he reached up and turned the key in the lock behind them, testing the handle to make sure it couldn't move.

"Filtiarn, what are you doing?" Conner asked, his eyes narrowing. Tension crackled over his nerves, freezing them in place as his stomach sunk. *I have a very bad feeling about this.* Filtiarn turned round to meet his gaze, but sharply looked away. He rose up, cracking his neck and striding across to the red leather chairs in the centre of the room. Leaning down to pick up a pair of black gloves, he pulled one on, turning his back to Conner and Demitri.

Conner's head spun as the situation dawned on him. Swallowing hard, he croaked, "Filtiarn? What the fuck is going on?" Demitri stood up beside him, clutching tightly at the knife by his side as his fangs grew in length.

"Please sit down, Conner," Filtiarn asked smoothly, gesturing towards the spare chair. He twisted around with a heartless smile, his eyes gleaming like silver pennies at his twin's distress. "I understand this must be confusing. Please allow me to explain it to you." He waved his hand once again, but Conner shook his head, folding his arms over his chest as he glared back at his brother. Filtiarn sighed heavily with a shrug, seating himself heavily and reaching over for a decanter of whiskey.

"You always were the stronger one, Conner. But you were made weak because of Erin, weak because of your nature. You could have been like me. You could have embraced your nature—instead you hid away in the shadows, 'watching over humanity'." He shook his head, his face expression growing dark. "Erin should never have been with you. She was meant to be a ruthless Alpha, a bloodthirsty werewolf, beautiful in her ferocity. But you hemmed her in, let her be soft and gentle. Ultimately, it allowed my mother to put that curse on her. If she had only chosen me...together we would have ripped apart this country." He laughed coldly. "Still, I suppose she did choose me, in a way. When our mother put that enchantment on you, it worked perfectly, and 'Filtiarn' brought Erin along for the ride."

Conner's face reddened with his fury as he glared down at Filtiarn. "I *was* the stronger one, you're right. You were weak because you couldn't fight your bloodthirsty nature. You think I didn't have moments where I wanted to be as my instinct commanded? But I didn't. You couldn't, because you were not strong enough. I saw that we had a higher purpose than to simply gorge ourselves on the humans oblivious to us. And what the hell is this about Erin? She is my mate. Always was, always has been, and always will be."

There was a squeak of leather as Filtiarn rose

gracefully, shaking his head as he tucked his hands into his pockets. "You knew I loved her. You didn't even notice how beautiful she was until I pointed her out. Then you only had eyes for her, and you stole her away from me."

Conner gritted his teeth, the hands falling from his chest and to his sides, where his hands coiled into fists. "I didn't *steal* her away, Filtiarn. She never went for you, because you weren't her mate. The first time I looked into her eyes, I wanted to protect her, to be a better man for her. You were only interested in what you wanted, and she knew it."

Demitri cleared his throat, interrupting, "So, Filtiarn...you created all this devastation and loss...for Erin? Because you wanted something you couldn't have?" The Russian jutted his chin proudly as he added, "Let me tell you something. Without the curse that was placed on her by Rosa, she is the best Alpha our pack could have. Because she isn't like you. She sees the good in people, and she cares about humanity. She never took watching over them lightly, never saw them as playthings like you did."

Filtiarn twisted on his heel, giving a low growl. "It was *not* just for Erin. She is my main priority, it's true, but this is about more than just that. Do you think I want my mother around anymore than he does?" A finger was jabbed towards Conner, trembling with anger. "I want that bitch *dead*. She's caused me nothing but strife, as well as Conner and Erin. If she had put the enchantment on Conner, I could have handled that. But when she cursed Erin...that was the final straw." His face lit up with a cruel grin. "Besides, I need her out of the way, so I can take my place as the rightful Alpha of the pack."

Conner snarled, lunging forwards for his twin. Filtiarn side-stepped him neatly, leaving him to crash into the wall behind. Conner righted himself in time and spun around, letting his claws slash out with blinding speed, fixing Filtiarn with a cold glare. "You will never be Alpha, and you will *never* have Erin. This ends now, Filtiarn."

Filtiarn gave an exasperated breath, knocking back a tumbler of whiskey. "Much as I'd love a chance to rip your face off, dear brother, I'm afraid I have bigger plans for you." The door opened with a loud click, as someone undid the lock on the other side, and eight of the tall guards stood in the doorway, unblinking as they focussed on Demitri and Conner. Filtiarn gave a grin. "I'm afraid you're going to be locked up for a while, as I have other visitors to meet. Namely your Erin, who is on her way here now as she follows *your* scent. Thank you for helping me with that tiny part of the plan, Conner."

"NO!" Conner roared as four of the guards grabbed his arms, dragging him back into the passageway. He struggled to free himself from their grip, but it was no use. He felt a sharp jab in his side as something was injected into his body, and he howled in fury, pushing his body to turn before it took hold. The world swayed around him as his vision blurred into black dots. The last image he saw behind his eyelids before he went cold was Erin, crying out for him.

Chapter Fourteen

In the bright daylight, the woods didn't seem quite so fearful. They seemed the last place anything bad would happen. Erin moved slowly through the trees, her boots making almost no sound on the soft green grass and muddy ground.

A cold wind picked up, playing with Erin's loose hair, making her automatically reach for her sword. Glancing through the trees to her right, she could see the clearing where they had sat the previous night, the fire that had been left now dwindled down to just a few tiny pillars of smoke. Staring at it for just a few moments longer, she made her way past, hoping to find a few clues as to what had happened to the others. She sniffed the air, but all she could smell was fresh, clean air, combined with the acrid smokiness from the remains of the campfire.

A sound came from before her, and she snapped back with lightning-fast reflexes. Someone was coming straight for her, crashing through the whispering grass with long, unsteady strides. Crouching down as far as she could, she reached for Sioctine with her left hand, sliding it free of its sheath. The sounds showed no sign of stopping, and Erin heard ragged breathing coming from the figure. She frowned to herself. *Could it be one of the others? I don't recognise the scent.*

"Erin? Erin, is that you?" a small voice came, from beyond the grass and trees, a childish voice. Peering, Erin raised her head until she could make out the form of Flo.

Flo noticed her before she pulled back, and came running over, a trickle of blood sliding down her forehead. As Erin narrowed her eyes and slid Sioctine out in front, Flo stopped short, breathing heavily as though she had ran for a long time. Erin drew herself up carefully, fearful of the trap that had been set, but prepared to fight.

"Erin! Thank god you're here! The others—we all got separated. Amber ran off, I've been trying to find her."

Erin tilted her head, glaring intently at Flo. "You've been looking for the others?"

"Yes." Flo fell quiet, and stared up at Erin with confusion crossing her thin face. "Erin, what's wrong?"

She doesn't realise that we found Jenny, or that she's alive. She thinks I still believe she's with us. Bitch. Clearing her throat, Erin asked innocently, "Nothing, where have you been looking?"

Flo jabbed a finger behind herself, deep into the woods. "There were some men. They dragged Jenny and Matthew off into this big manor house. I don't know what happened to the others. We must go and rescue them!"

Erin nodded, her eyes calm and serene. "Yes, of course. Where is this house? Tell me exactly."

Flo shook her head, grabbing Erin's sleeve and yanking on it. "No, come on. I have to show you it, now!" She began to run, but Erin stood firm and pulled her sleeve back. Flo glanced back, her mouth falling open, and frowned. She slowly turned and shook her head, placing her arms coyly behind her back. "Something *is* wrong."

Erin sighed. "Okay, look. I've had a weird night, Flo, and everyone—as you said—has disappeared. I can't just go running off into the woods unless I can be sure I'm not going to get more lost. I need to know how to get back for the others if anything goes wrong, that's all."

Flo searched Erin's face for a moment, as if

looking for any signs of untruth, but Erin kept her expression as emotionless as possible, despite her insides churning. Flo nodded slowly. "Okay, it's about half a mile that way. The trees give way to smaller trees, and then you'll see a big manor house made of grey stone. That's where they are."

Erin nodded in return, following the line of Flo's sight, making a note of the direction. "Oh, by the way," she muttered, as she slowly brought Sioctine up to flash in the sunlight, "Jenny will be fine. She healed very well."

As Flo turned her head to look at her and work out what she meant, Erin smiled cruelly at her in response. As Flo's eyes filled with understanding and her fangs slid out, Erin darted forwards and slid Sioctine between Flo's ribs. Fixing the lycanthrope with a furious glare, she heaved Sioctine back towards herself. She pulled so hard that Flo was shifted from where she had been pierced, dragging her across the grass until she slumped onto her knees, clutching at her side with a wheeze of breath. Erin raised Sioctine high above her head, swallowing back her instinct as it screamed for her to not hit the girl, despite what had happened. *Damn her for looking like a child.*

"It's no good. You and your friends are dead anyway," Flo hissed, her childlike eyes transformed by the spitting fury of a women, a strangled grunt following her words.

"Funny, so are you," Erin whispered, bringing Sioctine down with a hiss of air. There was a loud snick as metal cut through flesh and bone, and Flo's horrified face rolled free from her shoulders, her head finding its place amongst the weeds and undergrowth of an oak tree. Erin stood up, sweeping her hair back up, and wiped the perspiration from her forehead. She stepped back and let out a heavy breath, blinking rapidly to hold back the sting of tears behind her eyes. *I'm really not built for this. Not yet. Damn her, and damn her sister—if she even is her sister.*

Pushing her bitterness at the situation to the back of her mind, she whispered a quick prayer to the gods for Flo. Sliding her sword back by her thigh, she crouched down once more and edged in the direction that Flo had pointed in. Her nerves tingled, keeping her on alert. She had no doubt that if Flo had been wandering round, so too would her sister be searching for her, not to mention others.

Sweeping long, fresh grass out of her vision, almost gliding her feet along the moss below, she finally caught a scent that she recognised. *Conner. By the gods, Conner! Please be alright, my darling. Please be alright.*

Gulping in the air around herself, as if to capture his scent and imprison it within her lungs, she picked it up again and closed her eyes in pleasure, letting it wash over her. The scent led along the same path she crawled along. As if an invisible thread was leading her, she followed confidently, breathing in more and more of the musk that grew stronger as she neared the building.

As she looked upwards, her gaze met with an enormous stone manor reaching into the blue sky above. Several guards were walking about outside, talking rapidly to two others stood outside the front door. They wore black clothing and dark hoods, their faces hidden from her. Several more of them sprinted around the back, shotguns slung over their shoulders.

Silently as she could, she crawled around to check if there was another way around the back. As she skirted past, she noticed several more guards standing around a sewer grate at the side of the house. *That's how he got in. But if they're looking for him, that means he hasn't been found. Good news. And hopefully the others are there too, I know he didn't go alone from our camp.*

A knot tightening in her stomach, she continued on her path to the back of the manor. As she came into view of the rear, she saw that it was covered by four or five guards, all marching about in a patrol. She sat back on her heels for a moment, trying to think of a way to get in, when luck came her way.

Very close to where she crouched came one of the guards, clearly female, and unaccompanied by anyone else. The other guards were paying no attention to her, and she was far enough away from them to not be noticed if she walked off. Thinking quickly, Erin scrabbled around her for something heavy. Her fingers met with a fairly large rock, and she gripped it tightly. Holding her breath, waiting until the guard had just passed her, she mentally counted to three and threw it into the woods just beyond, deep enough that none of the other guards noticed.

The female werewolf noticed, and glanced up sharply, sliding her shotgun from her shoulder with a practised grip. She strode into the woods carefully, barely crunching the leaves below. Holding her breath, Erin peered over at the other guards to check that none of them had noticed, before silently following the woman.

The guard continued further in, scanning the area to either side of her, pointing her shotgun straight in front. Erin kept close behind her, staying hidden within the trees until the guard had made her way far enough into the woods to be hidden by the trees. As silently as she could, Erin slid her sword out, gripping it firmly in both hands as she edged forwards.

Just another step.

As Erin came forward, concentrating on the angle of her sword, her foot crunched on a leaf. The guard swiftly turned around, raising her shotgun in shock.

Before the guard had a chance to shout or shoot, Erin brought Sioctine swinging around herself, neatly snicking off the guard's head. She sucked in a shaking breath, working quickly, pulling off the guard's armour and hood. She recoiled briefly as the head lolled towards her with glassy eyes, but dressed herself in the black gear, hesitating for a second as she pulled the shotgun over her shoulder. Sioctine was still around her waist, hidden by the black cloth of the armour. It consisted of a black jacket, panelled at the front, back, and sides, and black trousers, which luckily were loose enough for Sioctine to slip in unnoticed.

Moving fast, she scooped up the guard's head and body, pushing them both into a large pile of dried leaves. She tumbled leaves over the corpse in an attempt to hide it, willing her hammering heart to slow down. *If they hear my pulse, it won't matter what disguise I'm wearing.* She turned smartly after satisfying herself the guard was hidden, and strode towards the manor, holding back the urge to run towards it.

As she came back into view of the manor house, she nearly jumped out of her skin when another guard appeared next to her from the trees. The male guard glared behind her into the woods before nodding back at her. He jerked his head towards the clearing within. "Anything there?" she heard his gruff voice ask, muffled by his hood.

She shrugged and shook her head, making no more than a noncommittal noise. She hoped it would be enough to answer him. She held her breath as he continued staring at her, squeezing her palms tightly, before he grunted at her. "Fair enough. Keep an eye out. She'll be by soon, I'm sure."

Erin nodded in reply, watching as he returned to

the side of the house. Taking a deep sigh of relief, she made her way over to the back of the house, towards the small back door. Three of the guards were gathered around it, and they stared at her as she grew near, ceasing their conversation. She cast them a quick look, glad they couldn't see through her hood, and motioned towards the door. Two of them moved in front of it, as the other guard marched towards her, slipping his rifle from his shoulder to his hands. He shook his head firmly. "No one is coming through right now. We need to stay outside."

Erin tutted. "Look, I really need to get through."

The guard shook his head again, and Erin could almost feel him scrutinizing her through his hood. "No. What do you need to get through for, anyway?"

She leaned her head and steadied the shotgun on her shoulder. Lowering her voice, she beckoned the guard to lean in, and whispered, "Look, I have a message to deliver, it is of imperative importance. One of the guards," she took a quick sweeping look around, "is not one of us. I saw her getting changed in the woods, but she looks far more armed than we thought, and with more people around her than we predicted. I must get this message in, at once." She tried to make her voice sound more urgent, willing the guard to believe her.

The guard straightened back, thinking for a second before relenting with a sigh. "Okay. But be quick. If you are not back out here in five minutes, I shall know that something is wrong."

"No problem, I shan't need any longer than that." She shoved past the two other guards, casting them a disdainful look.

"Get out of her way, let her pass," the other guard uttered, waving his arm. The two other guards cast one last stare at Erin before slowly moving apart to let her pass. She nodded curtly at them, and pushed the back door open, disappearing inside.

She found herself in a large lobby, surrounded by heavy mahogany furniture and vases of dried flowers. On all the walls above her, stuffed animals and their heads snarled down at her. Just looking at them made her feel physically sick. She had never felt too good about stuffed animals before she had been awakened to who she was, and she hated it even more now.

Dim wall sconces lit the way through the lobby, leading around the corner to even more passageways. *This place is like a bloody Tardis. Bigger on the inside.* Hearing voices coming down the corridor to her left, Erin decided to take the right-hand one, darting sharply into a dark corner. She waited breathlessly until the voices disappeared again, fading away into nothing.

Breathing out heavily, she peered out from the doorway and scanned the corridor. A great long green carpet rolled its way down the passage, lit by the dim electric lights. The walls were covered in gilded cream wallpaper, and crystal chandeliers hung along the carved ceilings. Erin sniffed eagerly, catching a mild fragrance of Conner's scent. *He's here. And...hmm...and Matthew too. And someone else I don't recognise. I think.* She frowned to herself as she concentrated on it, something sparking off in her memory. The scent was unfamiliar, but a twinge in her stomach told her that maybe that wasn't true.

As she roved her gaze down the corridor, her sharp eyes spotted a door partially open to her left, the room within dark. Taking a quick scan along the corridor, she moved towards the door, keeping herself pressed against the wall. Upon reaching it, she listened carefully, but could hear nothing from within. Cautiously, she pushed the door gently with her hand, allowing it to fall open.

She stepped inside, taking care not to make any noise as she took in the room. Nobody appeared to be there, the space empty. Flames roared in a great marble fireplace, lighting up the room with fierce warmth. Two red leather chairs were placed before the fire, sat upon a large Persian rug that looked a little threadbare, compared to the rest of the furniture in the room. The walls were covered with other portraits of solemn men and women, all with the same silver eyes. The far wall was covered in mahogany bookcases, filled with thick leather-bound volumes, some with titles written in languages she could understand, others in ones she didn't recognise at all.

Voices came to her once more down the corridor. Her heartbeat shot against her ribs, and Erin looked around herself for somewhere to hide. A large cabinet at the far end of the room offered the only protection. Racing over to it, Erin opened the doors to find that most of the space inside was empty. Making sure quickly that she hadn't left any footprints or clues to her whereabouts, she dived into the cabinet, clicking the doors shut behind her. Even with the doors closed, it left a small gap between them which she could still see through.

Two figures marched into the room. One of them was a guard, but the second figure was turned away from her, allowing her only a glimpse of his figure. He was dressed in a smart black shirt and trousers, his hands covered with tight leather gloves. From the back of his head, she could see his hair was jet-black, and that he was tall, but not much more than that. As the guard spoke, she recognised the voice as being that of the guard she had bluffed her past outside.

"Sir, it means she is in the building. We have to *find* her."

The man raised his hands up in a calming motion. "Enough. We will find her, how far do you think she can get?"

"But, sir-"

"No more, I have spoken." He leaned in, lowering his voice. "And if she is not found, I will remember that you were the one who let her in. Understood?"

The guard's bravado wavered, and he trembled as he bowed his head in respect. "Yes, s-sir, we will find her, I-I promise you." He left the room, closing the door behind him quickly with a firm click.

The man sighed to himself, shaking his head. Erin wrinkled her nose as she caught his scent, the same scent from outside in the corridor. *Werewolf. Perhaps I do know him.* Folding his arms behind his back, he strode over to the roaring fire. Without looking down, he sat himself elegantly into one of the leather chairs, crossing his legs casually. He gave a dark chuckle, pyramiding the gloved hands together. "You may as well come out. We can talk now that the children are gone."

Erin froze. *Surely he's talking to someone else, how could he possibly know I'm here?*

"Yes, I know you are there, Erin. I can smell you from here. Quite potent, I must say, but you *are* an Alpha. The cabinet was built in the seventeenth century, and it has stood the test of time, but never has it had the Queen of Werewolves standing within it."

Erin's heartbeat halted painfully for a second, before resuming its staccato against her sore ribs, as she grimly relented. Creaking the heavy doors open, she stepped out onto the Persian rug, straightening herself with a proud jut of her chin. Then her eyes widened as she swore under her breath, casting her gaze over the figure.

Filtiarn?

It had been nearly two centuries, but the resemblance to Conner was too striking for it not to be Filtiarn. He grinned back at her, his silver eyes framed by the tousled black hair falling across his forehead. He jumped up with a swift movement, the chair groaning at the change in weight. "It's good to see you, Erin. I hope you remember me. Conner explained his little...predicament with my personality."

Erin swallowed hard, coaxing saliva back into her dry mouth. Her head swam as she stepped backwards, sagging against the wall as her back found the cool surface. Shaking her head, she managed to stutter, "Filtiarn? It can't be you...you're...you're dead. You died. After I sent you away." *Holy fuck. What if he wants revenge for that?*

As though reading her thoughts, Filtiarn gave a shrug as he sauntered across to her, replying, "To quote Twain, rumours of my death were exaggerated. My mother decided she wanted to take over after you left, and she brought me back into the pack—not that many of them knew, of course." His silver eyes darkened to gunmetal as he added, "I don't blame you for sending me away, Erin. You did what you had to for the good of the pack. I always admired that, you always knew just what to do when the situation called for it. A true queen."

Erin's hand went to her side and her sword, her chest rising and falling with desperate breaths as she flicked her gaze to the door. *Can I run past him in time? We're probably evenly matched for speed, I could do it. Or kill him here and now. If he's working with his mother, he's not one of the good guys.*

Filtiarn followed her gaze, smiling wryly towards the door. "You can try it, Erin, but I wouldn't advise it. I've waited a long time to find you again. And nothing will upset my plans this time."

"You mean your mother's plans," Erin scoffed, her eyes burning with fury as the situation seeped in.

She narrowed her eyes as his face fell at her words, the smile disappearing into an ugly scowl. He gave a snarl. "My mother isn't as much in charge of the situation as she thinks she is. In fact, I'm on your side, Erin. I want to rid the world of her evil as much as anyone."

Erin laughed dryly. "Oh, I'm sure. What the hell would your motivation be for that?" Her grip tightened on the hilt.

Filtiarn's eyes widened as she spoke, as though she had asked a question she should already know the answer to. He rubbed a hand across the back of his neck and chuckled. "Well...my motivation is you, Erin."

Her blood turned to ice in her veins as she stared back at him, her mouth drying up once more into a desert. Her stomach squeezed against her insides, and she felt a black hold opening up somewhere in her mind. *This can't be good.* Wishing she hadn't backed herself into a corner of the room, she whispered, "Me? Why would I be your motivation?"

"Oh, Erin. Don't be so naïve," Filtiarn hissed, closing the gap between them with a single step. He gazed down at her with a wide grin, reaching across to pick a single strand of hair away from her forehead, stroking it back into place. Erin flinched at the movement, but stayed her ground, glaring up at him defiantly. "I've wanted you for as long as Conner has. But he was always stronger. Always the better-looking one, even if we were identical. The *good* one." His voice cracked on a bitter note. "What hope did I have of catching your attention, when I was so flawed next to him? But then...my mother explained the spell she put on both you and Conner. And when you thought he was Filtiarn, you loved him."

"That's the point, it was a *spell*. Not a real feeling," Erin protested with a furious snarl.

Filtiarn shook his head, leaning in and breathing deeply, closing his eyes as though her fragrance captured him. "That's where you're wrong, Erin. You see, a spell only works if there's that tiny, deep-down seed that will let it grow. Conner always wanted to allow himself to be free to explore his vicious nature, which was why he slipped so easily into my personality. And you..." His eyes lit up as he held her in his gaze. "You fell in love with him, because deep down, you wanted me too. Just as much as Conner."

She backed up against the wall, trying to ignore the pleased growl from Filtiarn as he hemmed her in, his musky scent washing over her. Erin's stomach twisted with the need to push him away, and the conflicting desire not to touch him. He pressed himself in hard, leaving nothing but breathing space between them as he fixed her with his glowing silver eyes. "You really shouldn't be so uncomfortable with me, Erin."

She let out a hard laugh, grateful for the cold press of Sioctine hanging by her side. "I'll remember that the next time I'm up against a maniac. I'll pass, thanks."

Filtiarn delicately raised one dark eyebrow, chuckling as he moved one gloved hand from the wall to stroke down her face. She swallowed at the touch, snapping her head away. His dark hair flopped across his forehead as he leaned in close to her ear, his warm breath making her body respond against her will, the strands of jet-black hair tickling her skin. "Do you ever wonder if you chose the wrong brother, my Alpha?" he whispered in a heated rush.

"Never," she snarled in return, glaring back at him, her fangs sliding out with intended malice. "I do, however, wonder if I should have killed you that day I sent you off with your tail between your legs."

Before she could pull away again, Filtiarn's fingers clamped around her chin painfully, forcing her to look up at him with fury burning in her eyes. He dragged a thumb across her lip, smirking at the gasp his touch wrought from her. She snapped her lips shut as though to suck the sound back, but his eyes lit up with lust as he stared down at her. "Good to see you're still as antagonistic as ever," he remarked. "I would hate to seduce you without that fiery spirit. It's much more fun when you fight me."

"This isn't a fight, Filtiarn. This is a rejection."

He gave a pleased smile, letting his own fangs arch out in response. "No, this is uncertainty. It's scary to step off into the unknown, Erin." He pushed himself off, striding across the room. "My mother believes I'm helping her to track you and Conner down, to kill you both. Truth is, I'm really only going to kill Conner…and her. Then I will be the pack's Alpha." He spun on his heel, sending a heart-stopping smirk her way. "And you will be *my* Queen, Erin. If I have to enchant you again, I will. In time you will see how I was always meant to be your mate, not my brother."

"I'll never let you," Erin growled, unsheathing Sioctine and bringing it before her with a metallic ring, the blade glinting orange in the wild firelight from the room.

"I don't see how you're going to stop me, Erin. Your small band of warriors have been separated, Conner and Matthew are in my dungeons, and my mother is in the building right now. You can watch her execution, if you like." He grinned maniacally, racing across the room in a blinding blur of colour, knocking Sioctine to one side as he closed the space between them again. He pressed his body tightly against hers, and smirked as Erin let out a needy gasp.

She scowled at herself for letting her body react so eagerly to him. His resemblance to Conner was throwing her off, and it was twisting her up inside. Before he got a chance to move in further, she deftly twirled her blade in her hand and brought it up against Filtiarn's throat. "Move any closer, and I'll cut your head clean off," she hissed in warning, her voice wavering.

"I like this side of you, Erin. So feisty," he rasped, clutching her jaw in his palm and leaning down. Even as the sharp edge of Sioctine pushed against the delicate skin of his throat, he captured Erin's lips in a hungry kiss. She tried to shove him away, but he was relentless, forcing her lips open with his tongue. He was ravenous, demanding as he nipped her bottom lip with his teeth, growling as the taste of blood spread through their mouths. Erin gave a panicked cry, bringing her knee up sharply, but he shoved his leg between hers, moving it back and forth seductively as he placed his hands either side of her face, deepening the kiss.

To Erin's horror, heat pooled in her centre and spread through her limbs, turning her boneless in Filtiarn's grip. There was something dangerously exciting about the feel of his leather gloves against her skin, a tantalising glimpse into another darker, seductive world as his firm lips moved over hers with dominant fervour. *Stop it, Erin! This is not who you are, and this is not Conner.* Coming to her senses, Erin pushed the blade of Sioctine far enough to draw blood in a thin line around Filtiarn's neck. He broke away with a hiss of pain, narrowing his gleaming eyes in retaliation.

"You'll come to understand, Erin. Whatever you think of me now."

Her eyes narrowed as she glared back at him, years of fury and mourning for the lives she and Conner could have had together shining through. *Never.*

As Rosa walked in, she could instantly tell there was something off about the meeting. Filtiarn's face was cold and sinister, his voice sounded dark as he murmured, "Come in, mother." Even something about the way he had said *mother* made her stomach twist with nerves.

She smiled happily, taking a deep breath as she entered the room, closing the door behind her. The two guards outside never looked over at her, but she caught one of them giving her a sideways glance before gazing back in front to the wall. As she moved towards Filtiarn, he spun around sharply, narrowing his eyes. "Stay there. I have something to say."

Caught off guard, Rosa halted, her heart thudding against her ribs. For the first time in her long life...she was afraid of her son. Placing her hands behind her back, she called her magic to the surface, rubbing her fingers together as she waited for the familiar warmth. A jolt against her arms told her that the magic was held back, wards somewhere in place in the room. Giving a scowl, she snapped at Filtiarn, "Why have you got wards in the room? Take them off, at once!"

Filtiarn sauntered towards her, each of his footsteps echoing against the wooden-panelled walls. He laughed coldly, shaking his head. "No, I'm not going to do that, mother. And you'll find the door locked. You see, I want to make sure you don't try any trickery on me when

I carry out my plan."

Rosa raised her eyebrows, fury burning into her eyes. "What plan? What are you talking about?" she demanded.

"You see, you've worn out your use to me, mother. I no longer believe you are the right wolf to lead the pack. *I* am. Which means I need to get rid of you. And worst of all..." he paused, to let his words take effect as he chuckled, "you tried to kill the woman I love."

Rosa's blood went cold as the impact of Filtiarn's words hit her. She swallowed nervously, clawing her hands as she prepared herself for a fight. "You little bastard. I knew you held feelings for Erin, and I told you to forget her. All you had to do was what I told you to."

"Fuck you, and your grand plan," Filtiarn replied coldly. "You have served yourself and only yourself. You were never interested in making me happy, or helping me to find another mate to forget her. All those years you kept me locked in your damn house until I agreed to help you. And it was all for you." He bit his lips, pushing his hands deep into his pockets and pacing back and forth. "And you thought I was your willing idiot, that I would do everything and anything you wanted. But I decided a long time ago that I would take power for myself, and claim Erin rightfully as my mate."

Rosa's body shook with rage as she spat, "And you really think Erin will fall at your feet just because you ask? You're a fucking idiot, Filtiarn."

He paused, grinning darkly as he spun back to stare at her. "No, but in time she will understand—with Conner out of the picture. And you, of course. It ends here, mother. Any final words?" To add emphasis to his words, he pulled his blade from his side, tucked away in the specially-made sheath he wore strapped to his leg. Closing the gap between them in seconds, he raised the metallic edge, hovering it under Rosa's chin.

She could see he wasn't afraid of her attacking him. Rosa knew she had no chance against her son. *I've relied on my magic for so long that I barely know how to use my fangs or claws anymore. I'm as weak as a newborn puppy.* "Yes," she hissed, her claws sliding out from her ring-encrusted hands. "I hope the lot of you burn in Hell. I hope you all destroy the world together, and pay a thousand times over for the crimes you have committed."

Filtiarn's eyes burned into gunmetal as he pressed the blade hard, drawing blood as she gasped from the sting it wrought. "A shame," he muttered. "I thought you'd have something more sarcastic to say, mother."

The blade moved swiftly, slicing through her neck as though it was butter. *Surprising, I thought it would hurt more.* All thought left her mind as her vision swayed and Filtiarn's head came into view. Then there was silence.

Chapter Fifteen

rin leaned her head against the cool stone behind her head, and closed her eyes. There was a small window —barred, of course—at the side of the cell, about eye-level with her. When she stretched up to have a look outside, she could only see an overgrowth of weeds and grass, expanding out into fields. The room was about six-foot wide, with a thick wooden door bolted at one end. Small tufts of grass poked out at the corners of the building on the inside, and a trickle of water cascaded down at the far end from the roof, pooling into a dark puddle in the far corner.

At least they left me with Sioctine. Not that they would have been able to remove it, of course. She guessed that they might have tried, but the enchantments were still too thick for them to even pull it an inch away from her. She hoped something nasty had happened to the guards as they tried. The floor was cold and uncomfortable, and she had to keep jumping up and shifting every few minutes to stop it getting numb, despite her tiredness. She sighed, dropping her head forwards into her folded arms.

"Erin, please look up."

Erin pulled her head up sharply, readying herself for a fight as she heard the strange, breathy voice. As she glanced up, a low breath left her open lips. Floating off the ground like a ghost stood her mother...Morriwyn. She wore a long, simple white gown, long tendrils of dark hair rolling down her back. As Erin stared at her, the stone prison around them melted away, and became a strange, dark forest, all the trees lit from within by a pale, ethereal light. Erin staggered to her feet to speak, but Morriwyn glided across, holding a finger to Erin's lips.

"Sh, my daughter. I know what you are going to say. I understand you are sorry for what has happened, but I also understand it wasn't you, I know you have tried to put things right."

"I know, but it's all gone wrong, and now Conner is—"

"It's going to be alright. You must know by now that nothing would separate Conner and yourself. Not even his brother." Morriwyn drew near and placed her hand on Erin's cheek, gently stroking it. Erin closed her eyes at the touch, warm tingles of electricity tracing the places her mother's ghostly fingers went. Morriwyn gave her such a radiant smile that Erin couldn't help but smile back wryly, realising it was such a long time since she had that the muscles were stiff. *"My Erin, you've had so much to deal with in your life. But everything you've had to deal with has strengthened you, for this moment. I'm going to have to ask you to make a very brave choice, and do something very hard. Will you do this for me?"*

Erin gazed up into her mother's eyes, feeling truly safe for the first time in her life. Her bottom lip trembled as she held back fresh tears, flickering memories of her mother laughing and hugging her flashing in like aged photographs. Her soul ached to have her mother by her side once more, to feel safe. *It's been so long since I knew what it was like to have my family around me. Conner and I have been alone for so long.* "Of course, mother, anything. If I need to do something...I...I trust you."

Morriwyn nodded in approval. *"Good. Then I will*

prepare something for you. Please wait here, I won't be long."

A whistling wind appeared from nowhere, a soft, yet powerful gust that made Erin close her eyelids against the force of it as it stung her eyes. When she opened them again, the woods and Morriwyn had disappeared, and she was left with the stone cell once more. Groaning, she sat down heavily again, folding her legs up to her chin. *Great, now I'm having hallucinations.*

A soft, ethereal light glowed in the centre of the room once more, bursting and filling the room with a strange, dreamy feeling. There was a rush of air, and Morriwyn was before Erin again, her white gown floating around her. Her hair flew about her head, some of the strands curling into the shape of a crown, framing her pale, silvery eyes. *"I'm not a hallucination."* Morriwyn grinned down at her.

Erin leapt up, Sioctine's tip scraping against the cold slabs of the floor. "I didn't mean it, it's just with everything that's happened..."

"I know, my child. I have brought you something. Something even I have never held in my hands before, but you will now hold firmly in yours. It took a lot to convince the others that this was necessary, but they agreed. It will be needed at the end...when you make your choice."

Erin frowned, her bravery slipping at her mother's words. "What choice do I have to make?"

Morriwyn sighed heavily. *"I'm afraid I don't know. All I have been told is that you will have to make a choice. I do not know the outcome."* Morriwyn put her hand behind her, and brought out a gleaming object.

For a second, Erin's eyes were blinded by the light that emanated from the object. When her vision cleared, she could see that it was a small glass cone. At the base were intertwined silver vines, one of them wrapping and winding its way up the glass to the top, where it ended in three leaves twisting together. Within the opaque, milky glass, Erin could see tiny sparks of soft light flitting against each other, dancing and flying.

"This object is called the Orb of Darkness. You must use it to weaken Filtiarn, and…kill him."

"Kill him?" Erin double blinked. "Filtiarn is no match for both me and Conner. We don't need an orb of flying sparks. We need to be together, and in the open air. I can't fight him in a small area with others ready to grab me."

"Rosa is dead, Erin."

Erin gave a hard shrug. "So? I'm pleased she's gone, but I don't see how that changes things."

"Rosa came from a long line of very powerful witches, descended themselves from a goddess. The power that runs in her veins did not come into being until her parents were both dead. With her now gone, that power has gone to Filtiarn."

Scoffing, Erin shook her head, holding her hands out in a questioning motion. "I don't understand—surely it would go to Conner? He is the eldest, after all."

The air around them darkened with tension, and Morriwyn's silvery eyes melted into black as she shook her head. *"I'm afraid it doesn't work that way. The power goes to the one who killed her. Rosa killed both of her parents when she was still young, and Filtiarn knew this story. This is why he was so careful to make sure Conner did not kill her first. He will now be more powerful than he has ever been before, and you must be wary, Erin. He plans to curse you as his mother once did, and he is capable of it. This orb will allow you to temporarily strip him of his powers, but it will not last long, maybe a few moments."*

As Morriwyn spoke, she held the glowing object out to Erin again. Erin swallowed nervously, the energy from the Orb resonating with a force so strong it shook her body, even without touching it. She held her hand out to receive it, grasping it tightly. As she pulled it to her chest, the soft lights flitted about madly, as though they drew strength from her presence.

Morriwyn smiled down at Erin again, soft and sad, reaching out her hand to stroke her hair back from her forehead. As she pulled away, she gazed over her shoulder. *"Goodbye, Erin. I hope we will meet again."* She took a deep breath, chewing on her lips as though thinking of something else. In a quieter voice, she added, *"I am sorry I was not there when you need me most. I should have been, and for that I will never forgive myself. I should have been there for so many of the years I have been gone.*

Erin nodded with a grim expression, keeping her gaze on the lovely vision for as long as she could until it faded away, melting back into her small stone prison. The Orb still in her hand, she folded her arms around herself, squeezing her eyelids until the tears no longer pricked at her. *It's been so long since I've seen her. I don't even remember her that well. No wonder I've always felt so distant from the world.* Pressing her fingers into her closed eyes, she took in a shaking breath, trying to still her battered emotions. *I can think about this later. Right now, I have work to do.* She stood up and turned to look out of the small, barred window.

In the distance, Erin heard shouts and yelling. She strained to listen to it, but she could only make out a general cacophony of noise. The evening was settling in, turning the clouds above into abstract shapes of pink and purple, lit against the orange backdrop of the slumbering sun. Her stomach knotted up as she felt the start of something both great and terrible about to begin. The edge of a wide precipice, where they would all either fall to doom, or rise to glory. Her mother was right. She would have to make a choice.

For the first time in centuries, Erin fell to her knees and prayed to the gods, willing them to aid her in the coming battle.

Chapter Sixteen

onner snapped his eyes open in readiness. He lunged out, his hand meeting only air. As he blinked, his vision cleared, the opaque edges of sleep fading away. The cold wind slapped at his face, an icy shock to his senses. He twisted around as his palms hit cool blades of grass, and the cry of distant birds came to his ears. Conner narrowed his eyes as he took in the field around him, the setting sun high above no longer warmer enough to penetrate the shade of the trees. As he looked around, he could saw that Demitri was not far from him, leaning against a single tree.

He ran over, clutching his old friend tightly on his shoulder. Demitri's head wobbled as he blinked up at him, his eyes glassy as he mumbled, "They...they gave me something. It's weakened me, my Alpha."

Conner let out a heavy sigh, nodding vigorously. "Shush, old friend. It's okay, don't worry. Why the hell are we in the middle of nowhere?"

Demitri managed a weak shrug. "I'm not sure, but I have a feeling it's something to do with that." Conner followed Demitri's line of sight, over to the very far end of the field. His face froze as he scanned the horizon.

Row after row of black-armoured werewolves waited at the far end. They ebbed with a green glow, a clear sign of enchantment on them. All of them looked bloodthirsty and wild, a sign that they were prepared for a fight, even if they had no idea they were taking part against their freewill. His blood ran cold as he stared at them, silently taking it all in. It hit him that they were waiting for something.

A battle.

Conner growled to himself, his fangs readying themselves for a fight. "By the gods, Erin. Morrigan, keep her safe." Conner swallowed back a lump in his throat as he felt out for her, his heart pounding as he thought about the countless hours he had been pulled away from her. As he stared off into the horizon once more, mentally ticking off how many wolves stood waiting to rip Demitri and himself apart, he narrowed his eyes as a familiar figure strode in front of them in gleaming silver armour.

Filtiarn. Conner growled to himself, clenching his fists. *He dies tonight.*

The lock clicked to Erin's cold cell, swinging open to reveal three of the guards, two male and one female. They wore the gleaming black armour, but had removed their hoods. Erin assumed it no longer mattered to them if she saw their faces. The female guard nodded towards Erin, her moon-coloured eyes dark and unfeeling. "Come on. It's time for you to play your part."

Erin raised her eyebrows. "What, no needle this time? What hospitality. You can fuck off. I'm going nowhere with you."

The female's lips curled into a malicious smile. "You will if you ever want to see your Alpha again."

At that, Erin's face went hard. She reached to her side for Sioctine's hilt, the stone in the hilt glowing with a fire she had never seen before. "Fine. Let's go."

The guards moved aside to allow her to pass between them, her head held high. They fell in either side of her, marching rapidly along a winding stone passage. It passed other cells, yells and groans ringing out from inside each one as they swept by, no light penetrating their dark depths. The corridor arched upwards sharply, and Erin breathed in deeply as she scented fresh air ahead. Her pulse sped up as a rush of adrenaline zipped along her veins, her heart thumping in her ears as her lips pulled into a firm line. The fight was coming. She could feel it in the tension of her spine.

The door flew open as one of the male guards gripped the handle tightly, and a wash of cool air swept over her, blowing the loose strands of her hair over her eyes. Another guard pointed forwards as she made her way out into the late evening sun, leading her towards the edge of a large field by the side of the manor. Scanning the nearby area, she caught sight of several figures in the distance, and some that were closer to her left-hand side As she peered closer towards them, one of the guards prodded her in the small of her back, nearly making her stumble. "Get a move on, we haven't got all night," he snarled callously.

She spun around, growling at the guard as she let her fangs come to the fore. Something in her eyes burned at him as she replied, "You do that again, and you won't have any eyes to see out of."

The guards laughed at one another. Something about their laughter made Erin go cold.

They snatched up her arms, frog-marching her to the centre of the field, her footsteps sliding on the wet grass as they hurried her along. The sun had almost disappeared behind the soft, velvety clouds of dusk, just peering out at the scene that was playing out before it. As she got closer, she realised that the figures at the far end were werewolves, throbbing with a dark green glow. *I don't know why, but...I know they are my pack. I can feel it. But what's happened to them? Is it magic?* The connection Erin held to her pack was as tight her bond to Conner, and she would know them anywhere.

"Stay here," one of the male guards commanded in a gruff voice. The three guards strode off on their own across the field, over to where the other lycanthropes waited.

Erin shook her head at them. *Stay here? I doubt that.*

She turned to retrace her steps, hoping to find a way out before the others ran after her, but then she remembered the words of the female guard. *They have Conner. I can't leave yet.* As she downheartedly came back to where they had left her, Erin noticed the figures to her left again. As one of them stood up, there was something familiar about the way he looked —

"*Conner!*" she shouted. She sprinted towards him, her heartbeat pounding in her ears, her instincts on high alert. As she grew closer, he waved at her, shaking his head. Erin slowed down, watching in confusion as her brow furrowed. It *was* Conner, but he shouted something about not going near, about...his brother? Before she grasped what he was trying to tell her, the sunlight was blotted from her vision as another figure stepped in front of her with a smirk and gleaming black armour.

Conner twisted around at a loud noise, realising he and Demitri were not the only werewolves close by. He rose up sharply, tilting his head to sniff the air delicately, picking up the scent of thousands. His amber eyes widened as he looked behind, seeing that there were indeed thousands of werewolves, all waiting with fangs bared and claws out.

Conner felt a thrill run through him. They were not alone, after all. Catching the eye of a male werewolf with dark hair and piercing blue eyes in ripped jeans, he yelled out, "Who are you all? Why are you here?"

The werewolf blinked for a moment before running over, bowing low as he pointed towards the field. "My Alpha. We are werewolves from all across the country. We heard of what Filtiarn was planning, and were advised to come to your aid...you and Erin's aid."

"Heard how?"

The werewolf swallowed nervously at Conner's tense tone, and lowered his gaze. "By Morrigan. All of us have told each other the same story. She came to us in dreams last night, warning us of a battle that would change the world forever, greater even than the recent war. We know you and Erin were not yourselves, and that you have broken free of the curse upon you both." He waved his arm back at the crowd of lycanthropes stood within the forest. "We are here to fight by your side."

Conner gazed at the werewolf, running a hand worriedly through his hair. "But who were you led by? How did you find us?"

"I can answer that."

Turning on his heel at the familiar voice, Conner let out a dry chuckle. "Taraghlan. I might have guessed."

The blond-haired werewolf came striding through the crowd with a wry grin, his eyes lit up with anticipation, Jenny and Matthew following him closely. Conner cast a wary gaze over Jenny as he noted the amber glow in her eyes, the ready smile on her lips. *So, he finally did it. He found his mate.* Raising an eyebrow at the general, he retorted, "I might have guessed you would be here."

"Well, I couldn't pass up the chance to fight, could I? Not my style," Taraghlan answered with a laugh, catching Conner's hand in his arm and slapping his back in a comradely manner. Reaching back for Jenny, who stepped forwards into his arms, he added, "Jenny is now one of us, truly my mate."

Conner smiled down at her, placing a hand on her shoulder. "I'm glad to have you with us, Jenny. I only hope you are ready for the battle ahead."

She returned the smile, winking cheerfully, although he could hear her thundering heart. "Of course. Wherever Taraghlan goes, I go. After all, he's my good luck charm. He's saved my life twice now." Jenny looked up, pressing a quick kiss to her mate's cheek. "And whatever happened before. It wasn't Erin's fault, and it wasn't your fault. But you're both going to save so many. I only want to help." Her expression hardened with her words.

As Conner was about to reply, a loud shout made him twist around in alarm, his eyes searching for the source of the cry. Erin stood in the centre of the field, three guards walking away from her as Filtiarn strode over. She was turned away from him, staring towards Conner. He ran over, waving his arms. "No! Erin, get out of here, go! He wants to enchant you again, leave!"

Erin held firm as she glared up at Filtiarn, drawing her blade between them. "So shall I kill you here and now, or shall we make a show of it?"

Filtiarn chuckled and gave a casual shrug. "Erin,

you won't kill me. I told you before, you're mine. I've brought you here so you can finally be by my side as we slaughter those who would go against our rule."

She gritted her teeth as she took a step forwards, biting out, "You don't seem to understand. You've already gone against my rule—so I must slaughter you."

He brought his gloved hands up, as though displaying them to her, and slowly removed each leather covering with deliberation. Her heart fluttered in trepidation as Filtiarn revealed the reason for covering his hands. They ebbed and glowed with power, curls and whispers of colours she couldn't name. As he went out to grab her arm, she moved quickly, reaching into her pocket for the bulky object Morriwyn had given her.

She held the Orb up in the dim light, its sparks flying about wildly, shoving it towards him. Erin breathed heavily, willing it to do something. *What am I supposed to do with it?* To her relief, Filtiarn gave a snarl, throwing his arms up across his face as though to protect himself, and backed away.

"Where did you get that?!" he demanded, his voice cracked with panic.

Smiling for the first time since she was forced onto the battlefield, Erin waved it about in front of him, swaggering as she edged closer to him, Filtiarn still stepping away nervously. "This? Oh, just a little gift *my* mother gave me. It's nice how we get things passed on from our mothers, isn't it?" She jerked her head to his hands. "I'm going to strip you of your powers, Filtiarn, and enjoy every moment of it."

"Damn it, Erin! You're going to ruin everything!" he roared. There was a moment of hesitation as he glared down at the glowing cone of energy, before he moved in a blur of motion, making his way back up towards his troops. Erin spun around, expecting to run after him, when the ground shook as though an earthquake was coming.

She gazed upwards in confusion, her senses momentarily lost as she tried to figure out where it was coming from. Turning her gaze up towards the hill, Erin's eyes widened and her grip tightened on Sioctine as hundreds of enchanted werewolves thundered down towards her, their weapons raised as warcries rose into the air.

Chapter Seventeen

[S]omething snapped inside Erin as she watched the lycanthropes running towards her, something primal and old. As she watched, it was as if everything around her slowed down. The enchanted werewolves running, the werewolves that flew out from the other side behind Conner to fight them, the very breeze slowed down into slow motion.

She felt very calm. Oddly calm. As though she was the only one who was in control, and she could do anything. *Is it the Orb?* She twisted and caught sight of Conner shouting at her to leave, and she smiled to herself. *Leave? Just when the fun's starting?*

She drew Sioctine from her sheath, the metallic ringing sound echoing in her ears like a tuning fork. The gleaming silver blade had never looked so bright or beautiful, shining in the early moonlight. As she drew it up, she admired the carved metal, the smooth blade, the fiery and icy jewels that finally worked together in perfect union.

Her eyes narrowed as she turned to face the werewolves running from the trees, holding Sioctine high. There was a roar from the were-creatures as she raised it, her blood racing with excitement. Her face set with cool determination, she then turned to face the oncoming enchanted werewolves...and Filtiarn.

Conner watched Erin turn, thrusting Sioctine into the air, and he heard the roar of the werewolves behind him, wild with rage for the oncoming fight. His instincts roared to the surface to protect her, to race over and cover her from the onslaught of Filtiarn's army. He could feel himself turning further, his mind becoming dangerously bloodthirsty as his beast urged him towards his mate.

He leapt up, unable to control himself any longer, throwing his head back and howling. It was so long and loud, that even the other were-creatures fell silent for a moment before joining in, a cacophony of mournful wailing and howling. The sound sent a chill down his spine—it was so dangerous in its warning that even the enchanted lycanthropes at the other end of the field paused for a second, their faces paling.

He sprinted across the grass, the distance between Erin and himself closing as his instincts screamed for him to catch her up. She let out a noise somewhere between a sob and a laugh as he snatched her up into his arms, burying his face in her sweetly-scented hair as he ignored the rumble of feet pounding against the muddy ground. "My Erin! My Erin. You're safe. I have you," he mumbled into her shoulder.

As he looked up sharply, he met her silver eyes, their brilliance gleaming with a love that had outlasted centuries of history and war. Placing his hands either side of her face, as though they had all the time in the world, Conner bent his head to her lips and captured them in a soft, passionate kiss. She tasted of cherries and warm sunshine, and their tongues melted together as he poured every emotion and feeling he had for her into the kiss, willing her to understand the way he heart still fluttered when he saw her. She moaned against their mouths clashing, and he growled in return, clamping her tighter to him and deepening the kiss. *She's so soft and warm. Still the same girl I fell in love with so many centuries ago. And I'll love her forever more.*

As he lowered his head, Erin traced her fingers along his jaw, her eyes shining into his. "I'm yours, Conner, just as you are mine. It's the way it always has been, no matter what. And it will always be that way. I love you."

As the pounding of feet and warcries grew louder, the two of them turned on their heels and dropped into a sprint, full speed towards Filtiarn's werewolves, their pounding footsteps perfectly matched by the pack behind them.

As Erin ran, she spotted three figures to her right, running into the field from behind Conner. *Taraghlan! And Matthew, and Jenny!* Taraghlan and Matthew turned, Taraghlan almost grinning with delight as he drew his sword and fangs out, but Jenny...she was very different from when Erin had last seen her. Her small fangs slid out from under her lip, her eyes a mixture of amber and silver, then turning still taking effect.

Erin waved towards them, shouting, "I didn't think I'd see you here!"

Taraghlan yelled back, "Do you really think I would miss a fight?" He grinned and looked back at Matthew, who nodded in return with a grin, his stomach wound healed over. "Jenny is perfect! She came round a short while ago!"

Jenny smiled delightedly at Taraghlan mentioning her name, and cried, "I feel better than ever! I would highly recommend it!"

Erin chuckled to herself, humour seeming to be the perfect side dish for the battle. Now only a few hundred yards away, she howled and continued to race towards the oncoming enemy. She glanced over at Conner, pride swelling her heart in her chest. He was strong and powerful, and he looked every inch her Alpha. He turned his head and caught her eye, grinning wolfishly back at her.

Erin took one last gulp of clean air, steadying her left arm and swinging Sioctine back as she came eye-to-eye with the first of the enchanted werewolves. Guilt bit at her for a few seconds, the idea of fighting the very wolves that were her pack eating away at her, but she pushed it away. It was kill or be killed. But she had to fight her way through to Filtiarn. *Just try not to kill too many of them.* The werewolves wound down into slow motion again as she arched Sioctine forwards, a sea of green glow, silver eyes, glinting black firearms and metallic swords.

Her arm came down as a male lycanthrope went for her throat with his blade, neatly cutting off his head as she dodged to the side, his mouth moving noiselessly in shock as his head flew through the air, spraying around his body with blood.

Time snapped back into place as Erin recovered from the swing. She moved faster, spinning like a dervish as she got to work with Sioctine, the fiery jewel eating up the very essence from the creatures about her. Blood and magic mixed around the were-creatures, turning the air into a dark green cloud with fire running through it.

She heard a female werewolf running for her from behind, fangs bared back, screaming like a banshee.

Lowering herself from the rifle the woman pointed at her torso, she thrust Sioctine straight out, piercing the werewolf through her throat like a skewer. She drew her blade back, the woman screaming in agony as she collapsed to the ground.

As she rose back up, she noticed Jenny twisting the head of a vampyre, howling as she did so. *Bloody hell. She's good, considering she hasn't had any formal training. I guess the wolf runs strong though her now.* The thought vanished as Erin saw a werewolf behind Jenny, about to jump onto her with fangs bared. Yelling loudly, Erin pushed her way through the swath of creatures fighting either side of her, howls and screams and blood flying across her face, as she raised her sword and sliced him in half.

"Thanks," Jenny said breathlessly, nodding as she twisted around to stab her short knife towards another attacker.

Erin nodded and patted her on the shoulder, turning back to face the fight again. As she spun around, there was a great scream—not of pain, but of anger. She glanced up above the throng of creatures, and her view met with Filtiarn's. His eyes were wild, and the smug smile was wiped from his face. The scream of anger had come from him. Erin smirked as she realised he understood. He was going to fall.

Her target.

She dropped into a dead run, heading for Filtiarn as though a thread drew them together. He turned his head quickly, and spotted her.

He snarled.

Conner caught Erin's eye as she ran. His heart filled with pride as he saw the fearlessness in her eyes. She neatly sliced off a wolf's head as he charged for her, Sioctine giving a dangerous, warning gleam as she did. He nearly howled as he saw how well she fought, how boldly.

A glowing lycanthrope rushed for him, and he quickly moved his own blade, disposing of the creature with no more effort than breathing. He lunged forward as another came in for a counter-attack, and almost smiled as the lycanthrope looked up at him in shock before sinking to the mud below. He wiped the blood from his eyes, aware that the sight of the rest of the blood on his face would both entice and frighten the other werewolves. Demitri was by his side, leaping and chopping as he pushed through. His side was bleeding, the wound slowly closing up, the flesh knitting itself together.

Conner swung his blade through another lycanthrope to the side of him, about to sink its teeth into the neck of a young female wolf. She nodded her thanks and turned to rip at another werewolf, making them cry out as she tore off his legs. As he glanced up, he dodged as a shotgun blast whistled past his ear. He turned back to look at the werewolf who had shot at him, his eyes full of lustful rage. The enchanted lycanthrope pulled back his shotgun to take another shot, but Conner got there first. He grabbed the werewolf under the chin, lifting him into the air, the man's legs kicking uselessly beneath him. Conner drew his claws out and crushed the lycanthrope's windpipe, his claws slicing through the skin and killing him instantly.

He heard a chilling scream from the centre of the field, making him gaze up for a second, as did the werewolf he was just about to thrust his blade into. It wasn't pain, it was fury. It was an ancient battle-cry. As he continued to look, he saw Filtiarn fixing his gaze on Erin.

Then he saw Erin, hesitating for a split second before running for his twin full pelt.

And Conner saw him snarl.

"No! *ERIN!*" Conner's pulse raced through his veins as panic flowed through his body, making him cold and numb. He tore desperately at the lycanthropes around him, shoving through them as he ran for her.

Erin saw the snarl, and chuckled darkly.

Just a few yards before she reached Filtiarn, something came flying at her, knocking her onto her side on the grass and leaving her winded for a second. Gasping for air, she raised her sword blindly as she turned to stand up again, when her vision cleared and she saw that it was Conner. She looked into his burning silver eyes, and smiled softly. She knew what he was thinking. She tried to scramble up again, moving in Filtiarn's direction, but Conner grabbed her again, spinning her about her waist as he held her. "Conner! Let me go!"

He held onto her tighter as she struggled. When he spoke, his voice was shaky and tight. "No, I won't! I'll do it, I won't lose you again. I won't." His voice trembled as he said the last few words.

Erin twisted herself around so that she was facing him, looking up into his blood-covered face. She put both her hands to his face, stroking his cheeks, her eyes desperately searching his. She saw fear—fear for her. Her heart pulled towards him, and she leant in, whispering to him, "Conner, I must do this."

He shook his head frantically, wrapping his arms tighter still around her. His warmth pressed into her, and she swallowed back the lump that formed in her throat at the loving embrace. "No, Erin, I will protect you this time."

Erin peered quickly over her shoulder, seeing Filtiarn sprinting away from her, slowly dicing his way through the were-creatures around him. Her heart racing, her brain telling her to run after him, she turned back to Conner and thought quickly. "Conner, listen to me. Do you remember a long time ago you asked me to trust you? To believe you?"

She would never forget that first meeting with him in the asylum. She understood the pain reflected in his eyes. After not seeing her for so many years, it must have taken all his will not to run to her. "Yes," he rasped.

She gripped his face tightly, bringing it closer to hers. "Now I must ask you to trust me. Morriwyn told me I must do this, do you understand? You must believe me! You must let me go!"

Conner took a deep breath, his eyes squeezing shut, hiding the hot tears that threatened to run from his eyes. He swallowed hard as he held her closer to him, pressing every inch of her against him, even in the midst of battle, as though they were alone. His grip finally loosened. Staring straight into Erin's eyes, he whispered hoarsely, "Alright."

Understanding his agony, Erin gazed for a second into his stunning eyes, knowing it may be the last time she looked into them. She pressed her lips against his, locking them in a desperate, hungry kiss. He met hers eagerly, and she swallowed the kiss, pushing it into her heart so it would never be forgotten.

Erin broke away, blinking back her own tears.

Then she leapt to her feet, and charged.

Filtiarn hadn't got very far, the werewolves

around him holding him back, snarling and clawing. Erin dived through them, Sioctine's weight feeling good and heavy in her tight grip. *My old friend. We've been through so much, haven't we? But this is the most important thing.* Feeling to her side, her fingers traced over the glass cone she had placed deep into her jeans pocket, the cold metal leaves kissing her hot fingers.

The wolves moved aside for her, turning to kill more of the black tide of lycanthropes either side of them. Filtiarn realised the were-creatures were moving, and twisted to look at Erin with a snarl, raising his sword. As it crashed down, she met it with Sioctine, thrusting back the crushing blow. He staggered back and laughed.

"Hello again, Erin. You had the chance to leave, but you chose to stay — all for your mate." He spat to one side as they circled one another, the werewolves on both sides falling back to leave them to the ultimate battle. They understood, every figure on the field understood, that the fight would not be won by the countless bodies on the ground. It would be decided by the two figures in the centre of it all. "Your *mate*. When you could have been my queen. You do realise you can't kill me?"

"Not true, remember?" Erin replied smoothly, moving quickly before he had a chance to slice his sword through her, pulling the cone from her pocket and allowing the glowing lights inside to flicker over his face. "This might help. You saw it before. You know what this is."

Filtiarn's face fell, his features turning pallid and white. His sword faltered, as did his voice, as he croaked, "Bullshit. You don't know what you're doing with it. How could you?"

Erin smiled wickedly. "You've upset a lot of people, Filtiarn. Seems even the gods want you to die."

Her face hardened as she spat out, "You would never be my mate, Filtiarn. I would never love you. Instead of forgetting me, you harboured feelings that would never be returned, you destroyed humanity, and now you're trying to destroy my pack. Did you really think your plan would work out and I'd fall at your feet?"

Before he had a chance to respond, she threw the cone towards him, taking a breath as she swung Sioctine high above her head. Yelling out a furious warcry, she brought the full force of her blade down, smashing the fragile glass of the cone as it rolled at Filtiarn's feet.

There was an explosion of light, a blinding seam of white that burned in its intensity. It threw Erin and everyone around her to the ground, including Filtiarn. A great beam of blinding light shot up to the sky, shaking the ground with the force of it. As she blinked to catch sight of Filtiarn again, he disappeared into white as he was covered in the burning light, a screaming cry ringing out from his vocal chords. As Erin watched, a black shadow emanated from the circle of light on the ground, growing in size, screaming to the night sky as it was pulled free of his body. The shadow shrieked a final scream, so piercing and shrill that Erin and all the werewolves around her covered their ears in agony. As it cried out, the shadow glided upwards into the beam of light, struggling and twisting as it was sucked up into the sky, disappearing with a blinding explosion.

Erin opened her eyes again, glancing over to where Filtiarn stood. He was still there, but he wasn't the same. He breathed heavily, gasping for air. His eyes were still silver, his skin paper-thin and bloodshot, but the whispering coils of magic were gone from his form. She smirked as she realised the cone had done its job. Filtiarn was no stronger than she was now.

He slowly looked up, straight into Erin's eyes with a burning rage. "*You*," he snarled, his fangs drawing out from his mouth. He sprinted towards her, shouting in his ancient tongue.

Erin ran towards him, steadying Sioctine. Her heartbeat thumped in her ears, her nerves crackling with tension as her muscles tightened for the thrust. The beads of sweat trickled down her forehead, the brisk breeze cooling her skin, the roars of all the figures about her heightening her readiness. She kept her gaze firmly fixed on Filtiarn.

As he raced towards her, Erin moved a split second faster than he did, sliding Sioctine down his blade. There was a scraping noise as the two blades met, but his stood still, as Sioctine glided down. Erin's blade met the hilt of Filtiarn's sword, and then his wrist. As she met Filtiarn's wrist, she pushed hard with Sioctine, watching intently as his hand and sword came away together, leaving his arm behind. Filtiarn's mouth fell open as his hand flew away, the sword spinning into the crowd of forces.

Erin pulled Sioctine up to his throat, and took a deep breath. "Any last words, traitor?"

"Yes." Filtiarn's tone was fearful. "If you kill me, you will kill Conner."

Erin laughed callously. "Really? And how exactly will that happen?"

Filtiarn's silver eyes met hers, empty and void of emotion. "Did you really think I didn't know there would be a chance you could kill me? You are the strongest among us. The Alpha of us all. A goddess who walks the Earth. I'm not stupid." He swallowed and gave a wheeze, blood pooling at the corner of his mouth. "Before I lost my powers, I cursed Conner. We are of the same blood, remember? When you kill me...the curse will kill him."

Erin's head swam as he spoke. As she kept Sioctine poised at his throat, she remembered Morriwyn's words. *You will have to make a choice...*

She glanced back over her shoulder, at her friends. She looked at Demitri and Matthew, and at Taraghlan, and his newly found soulmate, Jenny. All of them were fighting. For Conner and her. For them all.

Finally she looked at Conner.

His eyes met hers as she looked over at him. Centuries of love and longing washed over her as she gazed at his face. A feeling of completeness filled her soul, crying out to him. Memories of love and love lost came back to her in a rush, every moment from the shy young man who had bashfully given her flowers, to the strong man he had become, protecting her so fiercely. And she understood. She understood Morriwyn's words better than she knew she could. But she had to trust her. *Trust me, Erin.* As though he had read her thoughts, Conner nodded over at her. He rose up slowly, proudly giving her a smile.

Her eyes filling with tears, she turned back to Filtiarn. "The gods will never allow my mate to be ripped away from me. Even when your mother tried, we still found each other. And we always will. Talk to her about it when you see her in Hell."

She slid the blade through, cutting off Filtiarn's head.

Chapter Eighteen

s Erin split Filtiarn's head from his body, all the werewolves stopped in one collective silence of disbelief. Filtiarn's body stood for a second, before collapsing to the ground. His head bounced away down the small hill, spurting blood and sinew across the feet of the silent onlookers. His body fell with a thump, and Erin's heart eased. It was over.

All around her, the green glow floated from the lycanthropes dressed in the black armour, groaning and clutching at their stomach and foreheads as they keeled forwards. The air filled with cries and shouts as the magic left their bodies. The other werewolves raced to them with comforting words, helping them to their feet and shouting for water.

Her heart frozen in fear, Erin turned to face Conner.

He looked so calm, so happy. He smiled broadly at her, his eyes warm and amber once more as he gazed into her soul. Placing his hand over his heart, he whispered three words. The most important words. "I love you."

Then he collapsed to the ground.

Erin's blood ran cold as her ears filled with her own hideous screams.

Chapter Nineteen

rin ran faster than she had ever run before.

Falling to the ground, she grabbed Conner, shaking him by the shoulders desperately. "Conner, please get up!" she begged, her vision blurring over with tears.

He stayed silent.

"NOOOOO!" she screamed, her heart breaking in her chest. It burned her. She gazed down at his calm face and pulled his head into her lap, cradling it. The world swam and a loud buzzing filled her ears, blanking out the shouts and movement around her. "Conner, Conner, please! You have to wake...you have to!" A sob overwhelmed her, choking her for a second, tears falling freely down her face and splashing onto his cheeks. *I was sure Morriwyn would bring him back. I was sure of it. She told me to trust her. FUCK YOU, MORRIWYN!*

Erin was alone again. She had spent most of her life alone after Conner had lost her. Now she was alone again. Only this time Conner wasn't lost. *Lost means you could find them again. He's gone completely. Forever until I die.*

Nobody but the wind greeted her, slapping her wet, tear-filled face with sadistic glee.

"He's left me," she whispered, willing Conner to move. He made no response.

Erin clutched him closer, squeezing him to her chest. "No, no, you can't leave me...don't leave me alone here! I can't live without you, my darling. You are my everything." She frantically stroked her hands through his hair, closing her eyes and breathing in his scent, rubbing his face against her cheek. "Please don't leave me. I need you. I've always needed you. You're my heart, my soul."

She gently released her hold on him. Her insides were cold and empty. A shell. All that was left of her was a shell.

Her eyes fell on Sioctine.

The only blade that could truly kill her. The only blade she wanted to kill her. It was Sioctine's destiny. Always had been.

She turned to Conner, and smiled, stroking his hair lovingly. "I'll see you in a minute, darling." She bent over and gently kissed his forehead, so different from the heated kiss they had shared on the battlefield only moments ago.

She reached for Sioctine, bracing herself.

Conner felt very odd. He felt as though he was floating on water, and yet he felt as though his limbs had disappeared. The next moment he felt as solid as rock.

He played about with the sensations for a while, making his limbs go and come back again, until he realised he hadn't moved his eyes yet. They were still closed. He chuckled to himself. *Don't be such an idiot. Open them.* Prying them apart, he was met with a beautiful image. An enormous forest spread out beneath him, the lush green trees gently swaying in the soft wind, a warm, summery breeze. The sun was just setting, turning the sky into a rainbow of pink and orange. The shy moon peeped out, coyly waiting for its turn in the huge stage of the world.

Somewhere behind himself, he heard laughter. He

turned, but saw no people. Instead, he saw a pretty little row of thatched roundhouses, like those of the village from his childhood. A tall mountain stretched above them, protecting them from the wind, allowing the sun to warm the fronts and bath them in light.

He strode towards them, the smile never leaving his lips, when a strange noise made him halt. He frowned to himself, but shrugged when he heard nothing more, and continuing to make his way over to the houses.

There it is again! Someone was shouting. Conn? Conn...er? Was that him? He couldn't remember. *Is that my name? It sounds familiar.*

He turned around, and let out a low breath as he saw a tall woman in a white gown floating towards him. She had long dark hair, and fury was etched on her features, her eyes gleaming as silver as the moon above.

"Conner!"

Something clicked in his head as she shouted. *Yes, that's my name. I'm sure of it. And wasn't there someone else? Fil-something. And Er-something.*

"Conner, you must go back...you must!"

What is she on about? I'm fine here. Where am I supposed to return to? "Go back where?" he asked.

The lady grew more distraught as he asked the question, her hair flying around her head as though lifted by magic. "You need to go back to her! You need to remember! This is not where you are meant to be yet, Conner. Not without her."

Conner frowned. "Her? Who? And what am I supposed to remember?" He tried hard to make sense of the thoughts floating around his head —maybe they were what he was supposed to remember. But they slid away from him as he tried to fix on an image, slipping away like wet fish in his hands.

The lady sighed, a single tear falling from the corner of her eye. "You must remember...Erin! Erin." As she said this, she opened up an image in front of him, waving her arms. A wavering circle appeared, a mirror into another world. It was himself, laying on the ground in a moonlit field, with a beautiful girl crying over him.

In an instant, everything came back to him. The memories tumbled in, like a dam had burst with the sight of the image. He gasped in horror, the shock of it throwing him to the ground on his knees with an anguished howl. He remembered Erin, *his* Erin. He remembered her flying towards Filtiarn with her sword. He remembered Filtiarn falling, and the werewolves being freed of the magic around him. Then he remembered smiling at Erin before he told her he loved her, and he...*died.*

He shook his head frantically, jumping up and thrusting his hands towards the woman, his eyes wide with fear. "No, I can't leave her! NO!"

"You must go back." The woman told him, pointing to the image. "Quickly! There's no time!"

Conner glanced up fearfully to the image before him. As he lay still on the damp grass, he watched as Erin lifted her sword up, and pulled it towards herself.

"NO!"

Erin looked down at Sioctine. For the first time, she noticed that the jewels were not glowing. It was almost as if the sword was mourning for her loss as well. She stroke her hand loving over the blade. She had always been connected to the sword by her soul. When it was made, Morriwyn had created the very metal it was forged from by taking a piece of Erin's soul. It made it incredibly powerful in her hands, but it was also the reason for her enchantment over the centuries.

She glanced back over at Conner and took a deep breath, placing her sword in front of her torso.

"NO! Erin!"

Erin's heart skipped as the voice rang out, Sioctine slipping from her hands as she stared at Conner, her mouth falling open.

Conner gave a cough, blinking his eyes, and croaked, "Erin...I'm sorry for leaving you."

Erin stared at him for a second, not saying a word, no sound but the breeze. Then she leapt on him, sobbing and laughing at the same time. Her heart exploded with emotion, and her body racked with the force of it, pouring every inch of her soul into him as she embraced his form. She leaned up, and kissed him on his face, his eyes, his lips, everywhere. "Oh thank you! Thank you, Morriwyn! Conner, you scared me. Don't ever leave me again!" *I'm sorry for my earlier anger, Morriwyn. I knew you wouldn't let him leave me. Thank you...mother.*

Conner smiled warmly, closing his eyes with the sensation of her lips everywhere. He threw his arms around her, pinning her to him in a hug that told her he would never let her go again. He opened his eyes to see her smiling down at him, her blue ones filled with tears, the beast within pushed away, along with the silver eyes.

"Don't cry, darling. I'm here now. And I'm never leaving your side again." Conner stroked her cheek, wiping her tears away. She laughed happily, and kissed him on the lips again, pressing hers so hard that they almost bruised his.

He tried to sit, groaning as Erin helped him up. He felt his head with searching fingers, a gave a moan. "Shit. I think I must have taken a bang to the head, it's throbbing like hell."

Erin and Conner smiled at each other as the others crowded around them, all grinning cheerfully. The tension was gone from the air, like a bad dream that had passed. Taraghlan helped Jenny up from the ground, whispering to her lovingly as he pulled her into his arms. She was smiling, but weakened from the first battle she had ever been in. Demitri and Matthew were already up, helping some of the others around them to their feet from the damp ground. Jenny waved over to Erin from Taraghlan's hold, and Erin waved back, smiling.

For the first time in a long time, Erin felt as though she had nothing to worry about. Her hand closed tightly around Conner's, and he pulled her down to him in a searching kiss. She relaxed in his hold and melted into him, promising herself that they would never be apart again. Their love could outlast anything.

The group sat around a warm campfire, built up to a great height by the other werewolves. Many of them had decided to return home, to start helping the process of returning the world to the way it had been before the war. Others remained by Erin and Conner's side, sitting and talking in groups. Their new pack.

Erin thought back to the fateful day the battle had begun. Not when the war started, it was earlier than that. She thought back to the fateful moment Rosa had spat a curse at her, when Filtiarn was sent away. It seemed so very far away now.

She shook herself mentally back to the present, and gazed across at her friends with a warm smile. Jenny was sat on Taraghlan's knee, gently stroking his cheek. He had another scar there now, undoubtedly gained during the battle, but his face was softer. There was something about his eyes that sparkled, and his smile was broad as he stared longingly at Jenny. Matthew and Demitri were sharing stories about the battle, animatedly throwing their arms about and laughing every now and then, firm friends to the last. Conner was busy gathering some more firewood, but he stopped every few moments to run back and check Erin was okay, pressing kisses to her forehead. She grinned at the thought, her chest swelling with the love her heart contained for him.

Erin looked over at Taraghlan and Jenny, and asked, "Hey, guys. What about you two and Matthew? How did you know where to come?"

Taraghlan answered, still smiling at Jenny. "Well, this sleeping beauty still hadn't woken up for a while, but she came around, shouting something about you two needing help in a field somewhere. Matthew had nodded off in his chair, and he snapped awake shouting the same thing. About ten minutes later, a whole crowd of werewolves came past the houses, heading for here, and they told us the same story."

Erin raised her eyebrows, suspecting she already knew the answer. "But how did you know?"

Jenny giggled, and replied, "Turns out that every werewolf had the same dream. A lady in a long white robe, called Morriwyn. She came to us all, and told us that we needed to fight, to save you and Conner, and all of us." She looked back up at Taraghlan, her face growing solemn. "I felt like she was...like she was a mother to us in some way. Does that sound crazy?"

Shaking her head, Erin grinned. "No, not at all. That was my mother, but she's your mother too. The Mother of all Werewolves. I knew she wouldn't let me down. She saved us all." A shiver ran along her spine as she thought she felt the ghost of a hand trail along it in a loving gesture, but she didn't turn around. She smiled to herself as she closed her eyes in pleasure. *Mother. I can't wait to see you again. I love you so much. You saved us all.*

Jenny let out a low breath, chuckling. "I guess she did save us all. I'd be proud to call her my mother." She threw her arms around Taraghlan's neck, pulling him in for a gentle kiss. "And I've got a lot to learn about this lycanthrope thing. But I think I've got the perfect teacher."

Taraghlan grinned back at her, the hardness in his face that Erin had seen only a few weeks earlier gone forever. "And we have all the time in the world to learn. Together," he replied, stroking Jenny's chestnut hair with his long fingers before cradling her into his chest.

Erin nearly sighed at the love blossoming between them, happy to see them so in love. *Taraghlan waited a long time for his mate. And whether he knew it or not, I think Jenny did too. She's good for him. Speaking of mates...where's mine gone?*

As if answering her, Conner walked up behind her, clutching a large bundle of firewood. He dropped it next to the fire, throwing a few twigs onto the already roaring flames. He grinned at Erin, settling next to her. "Are you alright, darling?"

Erin nodded, throwing her arms around him. "Much better now I've got you by my side."

Demitri made a vomiting noise, jokingly. "Get a room!" he shouted over, making Jenny and Matthew giggle, Taraghlan chuckling as they looked over. But their eyes shone with happiness for their alphas, their lips curved into loving smiles. "For crying out loud, we're getting surrounded by couples, give it a rest! Some of us single guys want to talk about guy stuff."

Erin and Conner laughed in unison, Erin glancing over at Demitri's beaming face as she blushed, something she hadn't done for centuries. She almost felt like the young girl she had been back in her Iron Age village. Conner turned back to her, stroking a thumb along her jaw, "Shall we take a walk and let the others have some peace? We have to all get a good rest tonight before we get back to Athol Castle tomorrow morning. There's a hell of a tidy-up to do."

"Okay." Grasping hold of his hand, Erin pushed herself off the ground, falling into step with Conner as they strode a short way from the group. They walked through the contented groups of werewolves, holding each other's hands tightly as each lycanthrope grinned up at them and nodded their heads in respect. *Real respect,* Erin thought to herself. *Not born of fear, but born of love. It's the only kind of respect I ever want to feel again.* Conner leaned in and put his arm around Erin's shoulders, squeezing her closer.

They walked to the far edge of the large field, where the land dipped down, to look over the wild Irish countryside. Lush green trees swathed down the gentle hill, flanked by tall brown and green grasses. The large silver moon, now sitting in a clear, cloudless sky, beamed down at it all, illuminating the landscape. Somewhere in the distance, an owl hooted goodnight to itself, the sound carrying across the beautiful landscape. The trees gave way to the small village where Erin had hid with the others, its roofs looking like a tiled mosaic.

Conner pulled Erin in for another kiss, smiling gently as they pulled away, then turned to survey the landscape below with a proudly jutted chin.

Erin gazed up at him, tracing every line of his face with her eyes, drinking in every tiny detail of her mate. "I thought I'd lost you, you know. Promise me you'll never go away again."

Conner's eyes went soft as he turned back to her, filled with sudden intensity. He grasped her hand tenderly. "I promise you I will never leave you again. We are fixed together for the rest of time, now. Like glue." He sighed, and closed his eyes for a second, opening them again to Erin's blue eyes. "I thought I had nearly been lost as well. It was only thanks to your mother."

"My mother? Morriwyn helped you? She was busy, huh?"

A sly smile curled Conner's lips. Erin grinned back. *I like this happier Conner. It suits him.*

"Yes, she helped me. We owe a lot to her."

As Erin gazed out over the landscape, she hugged Conner closer, the feeling of his warm body against her the best feeling in the world for her. He hugged her in return, lacing his fingers through her hair and kissing the top of her head.

"Conner?"

"Yeah?"

"What happens now?"

"With what, darling?"

"The world, I guess."

"We have to sort it out again. We made a mess of it. Now we have to pick up where we left off thousands of years ago. We have to make sure that we look after humanity this time, just as we did before. We'll sink back into the shadows, as though we never existed. And they'll forget about us, in time. And we'll watch over them, as we were always supposed to. And this time, nothing will pull us apart again."

Erin sighed happily, grinning up at Conner. *I like that plan.* He leaned in, pressing his lips against hers, putting his hand behind her head and pulling her in, turning the gentle kiss into something more passionate. Erin responded eagerly, her mouth meeting his with the same intensity.

The two of them kissed lovingly, holding each other close, closer than they had been able to be for centuries, framed by the new world that they would help to form.

Chapter Twenty

iltiarn gave a groan as he rubbed at his neck, a throbbing ache settling into his bones and spreading along his body. With a flash of memory, he recalled everything that had happened in his last moments. Erin's speech. The scent of blood and sweat from the battlefield. The snick of the blade as it tore through his neck. The cold that entered him as the world spun to darkness.

Snapping his eyes open in a cold sweat, breathing heavily, he eased himself up into a sitting position. He scanned the area, his heart dropping as he found himself in the centre of a glade of trees, the branches moving together rhythmically above his head. The movement jarred him as he realised there was no wind, so sound. The sky above was pitch-black, filled only with twinkling stars looking down at him. As he pushed himself off the ground gingerly, wiping the grass from his hands, Filtiarn looked around for any signs of life. *This is my punishment. I'm to be alone forever, for wanting Erin.* The thought wrung sorrow from his heart, pricking his eyes.

A sigh came from behind him, and he spun around frantically, his heart thumping against his ribs as he readied himself to fight whatever came. Relief washed over him as she saw it was only a woman, dressed in a white robe with long, dark hair tumbling down her back in thick tendrils, her silver eyes roving over his form with cool indifference. Then the blood froze in his veins as he recognised her. *Morriwyn.* His eyes widening in fear, adrenaline still flowing through his body like acid, Filtiarn dropped to his knees before her, casting his gaze to the muddy ground. "Mother of all Werewolves."

"Rise up, Filtiarn. Let's not pretend that you've revered me all these years."

Her voice, although breathy and soft, held a note of warning. Nodding in reply, he eased himself up, cautiously gazing up into her eyes. Morriwyn glided forwards, reached out a hand to press it against his cheek. Filtiarn jumped at the movement, startled by how loving her touch was. She smiled at him, although her eyes still burned with fury, and she rasped, *"Filtiarn, I can never forgive you for what you helped your mother to do to Conner and Erin. But...I know that it was not all your fault. We cannot help who we fall in love with, and often our heart can rule our head. This last so much longer if we live beyond a human lifespan. But she was never your mate."*

The weight of Morriwyn's words slammed into him, and Filtiarn groaned from the force of them, his heart sinking. "You mean...I never found my mate? She was never meant for me?" His voice cracked. *My mate was out there, waiting for me...and I never found her.*

"I'm afraid so, Filtiarn. I feel for you."

He slumped against a nearby tree, running a hand through his hair. It was strange, every feeling he had ever held for Erin seemed to be gone, as though it had never happened. The only thing he felt was mourning, for the mate he would never know, and his wasted life. Raising his eyes again to Morriwyn's gentle features, he whispered, "Why don't I feel anything for Erin anymore?"

She raised her arms in a searching gesture, glancing from side to side. *"You died, Filtiarn. This is the Otherworld. When you came here, any attachment you had to anyone but your mate was washed clean, pulled away to prevent it happening again."*

He frowned deeply, shaking his head. "That doesn't make sense. It can't happen again, anyway. I'm dead."

A soft chuckle left Morriwyn's lips, tinkling like bells as it carried across the still air. *"That may not be...entirely the case. I have spoken with my mother, Morrigan, and she feels that perhaps you deserve something of a second chance."*

Filtiarn's soul leapt at her words, and he clutched wildly at the thread of hope dangling before him, letting out a harsh gasp. "A second chance? You mean...I can go back?"

A fragrance of flowers burst across the air as Morriwyn arched an eyebrow delicately, nodding her head as she sailed towards him again. *"Yes, but it's not that simple. You cannot expect to go without your punishment, Filtiarn. Although we feel that at least your punishment was metered upon you by the wrongdoings of your mother. We will allow you to go back, but there are terms."*

"What kind of terms?"

"You may return, but not to Ireland. We're sending you to America, to help restoration there. You will be far enough away from Conner and Erin that they may continue with their lives, but you will also be closer to your mate. But you will have to do a lot more than that."

My mate is in America? No wonder I never found her, I never went there. Filtiarn swallowed hard, bending his head respectfully, his palms sweating as he realised he was on the precipice of making right on everything he had ever fucked up in his life. "I'll do anything. Anything. I want to," he added vehemently, hoping she could feel the emotion behind his words. *I mean it. I messed up so much, and I nearly tore two mates apart from each other, whether by my hands or aiding another to do it. I'll burn in eternal flames if it gives me a chance to make up for that.*

Morriwyn gave a sly chuckle, tossing her hair over her shoulder. *"Well, there will be no flames necessary, Filtiarn,"* she replied, his eyes widening as she revealed she knew what he was thinking. *"And we know that you mean it. Your mother was a very powerful manipulator, and you were her greatest project. You may have been blinded by your feelings for Erin, but you would never have done what you did without your mother leading you on."* Her expression sobered, and she continued, *"We are sending you back, but you must atone by helping others. Humanity is crumbled to the ashes, and it will rise triumphantly from them, but not without help. There are many supernatural creatures who wish to take advantage of the situation, and without anyone stopping them, they will succeed. Humanity will live in fear until they are dealt with. You must hunt down these creatures and send them here, to the Otherworld."*

His hands curled into fists as he stared back at Morriwyn, nodding eagerly at her statement. "Sounds fair to me. How will I know these creatures?"

"You will know. Your instinct will guide you well. And those who seek aid will find you, whether through me or other means. You simply have to keep your eyes open and your heart ready. And..."

"Yes?"

"Your mate will come to you. She will find you, and you will recognise her. Don't expect her to know you straight away though, nothing worth fighting for is easy. Are you ready?"

Filtiarn smiled broadly, the first real smile he had felt ghosting over his lips for centuries, and nodded firmly. "I'm ready. And...thank you, Morriwyn. I will never stray again. But can I ask one more thing?"

"*Of course.*"

He bit his lip. "Will Conner and Erin be happy now? I mean, are they going to be okay?"

Morriwyn smiled warmly, the anger gone from her brilliant eyes and replaced by the love she held for all her children. "*Yes, Filtiarn. They will, as it says in fairytales, live happily ever after. Their love is stronger than any I've ever known.*"

Filtiarn grinned back at her, feeling a burst of happiness for his brother and Erin. *I remember I didn't always hate him for getting Erin. Before I was sent away from the village, I was...happy for them? I remember that. She became my loving sister-in-law, and I always loved Conner. I'm glad they will be happy without me around.*

He didn't get a chance to think further on his memories, as a strong wind wrapped itself around him. He gave a cry, reaching out for something to hold onto as Morriwyn smiled down at him, but the wind whipped so fiercely that his legs left the ground and he was carried off. It blinded him with a rush of white light, similar to the one that had stripped his mother's powers from him, and he gave a wheeze, struggling to catch his breath. There was a boom of sound, like a rumble of thunder inside his head, and he squeezed his eyes shut. Clapping his hands over his ears as though to rid himself of the sound, his stomach churning from the whirling tornado he seemed trapped in, he bit down hard on his lip and tried to steady himself.

"Ow! Fuck," he swore out loud as the wind dropped abruptly, slamming him onto a hard, cold surface. Snapping his eyes open, Filtiarn looked around to see he had landed in a dark, grimy back alley somewhere. Car horns and shouting could be heard off in the distance, and a cat screeched behind him, making his nerves jump. *Where the hell am I?* He shoved himself off the ground, pausing as the spin in his stomach finally lurched into his throat, leaning against a nearby brick wall to empty the contents off his stomach behind a dumpster.

As he wiped his mouth off with the back of his hand, he took in a deep breath. *I'm here. I'm alive. Morriwyn was as good as her word. And so I am I. Although I don't have a clue where to go.* Legs still wobbling from the sudden rush to earth, Filtiarn stumbled out from the alleyway, looking left and right as he scanned his new home. It looked much as Ireland had looked, with ruined buildings and crumbling walls dotting the horizon, but a dull orange glow settled over everything, the heart of a city. Straightening his jacket, Filtiarn blinked to glance at a nearby road sign, hanging between street lights at the entrance to the city.

Welcome to Boston.

Filtiarn grinned up at the words, feeling an inner peace he was sure he had never felt before. Pulling his collar high around his neck, he shrugged off the cool air of night, and tucked his hands into his pockets. Striding off towards the centre of Boston, he let out a contented sigh. *Time to get to work.*

And although this is the last chapter in the
Athol Trilogy, Filtiarn will return in...

THE WOLF
RETURNS

BOOK ONE OF
The Wolf's Atonement

Enjoyed this book? If you liked it, please leave a
review and let others know! Thank you.

The Athol Trilogy

Conner
Erin
Filtiarn

Other books by Miranda Stork

The Scarlet Rain Series

Vigilante of Shadows, Book 1
Keeper of Shadows, Book 2
Creator of Shadows, Book 3
Destroyer of Shadows (coming November 2014)

The Grim Alliance Series

Reaper's Deliverance, Book 1
**Promises of the Dead, Book 2 (coming
September 2014)**